AERTH

AERTH

Deborah Tomkins

WEATHERGLASS BOOKS

AERTH

For Ian, Alexandra, Christopher and Nathaniel,
with all my love

Contents

Listen with all your heart

Now we are seven

Had Magnus of Arden stayed home, enjoyed his party, blown out the seven candles on his cake, he would not now be sitting at the top of an oak tree, quietly observing like an explorer.

Through gaps in the bright early-summer leaves Magnus can see the farmhouse a quarter mile away, and beyond it the once-wide elm-lined high road, the machine dump – forbidden to all but a few – and the turf roofs of the village, solar panels gleaming scarlet in the setting sun. Surrounding all looms the wildwood, dense, dark, almost impenetrable. Here bears and wolves and lynxes prowl, and elk and moose roam the narrow paths which were at one time thoroughfares for humans but are now entangled with brambles, ivy and straggling, twisted shrubs. When he's older, he and Ryan will explore some of the abandoned villages, visit the old machines in the dump. If their mothers will let them.

People have gathered in twos and threes, milling about the garden and orchard, sipping from mugs of tea, glasses of cider. They arrive in pony carts, on bicycles, by foot. Voices carry far on this windless evening.

Magnus is hoping that the uncle who made his last birthday so exciting will appear. This man, somehow more vibrant and alive than anyone Magnus ever met before, had driven up on a motorcycle, laughing at everyone's surprise.

People stood back in a semicircle as he parked his vehicle, held their children's hands. Only Magnus was allowed to sit on the gleaming machine, his legs dangling, his fingers barely reaching the handlebars. His mother stood beside him, arms folded, her smile cautious, her brows drawn together. Then she shrugged, said, 'Behave yourself.'

Today Magnus understands that she meant her brother, not her son, judging from her comments this morning, even grumpier than usual: *Revisionist... Conspiracist... Dangerous... The world's moved on... And that machine, he'll kill himself on it one day...*

Last year his uncle's laugh was so infectious that even Magnus's mother smiled and seemed happy. Until he placed Magnus on the back of his machine and rode him on the bumpy track down to the weir. Then he was banished, her anger so fierce and uncompromising that nobody could calm her. Magnus is not to mention that man's name again, even though the dogs liked him, and dogs, they say, always know.

Lights have come on in the house. From lamps hanging along the fences little pools of brightness shine into the fields. The rising crescent moon is almost invisible in the eye-blue sky, and Magnus shivers. A sparkling summer frost is forming on the oak leaves and twigs.

The uncle hasn't arrived. But he might still, even though it's getting late. Magnus is sure this man makes up his own mind. And he said, last year: *This is your day, Magnus, nobody else's*, and although Magnus had understood him to mean he didn't have to share it with his twin sister who died when they were babies, he sees now that he shares this day with his mother too.

There's commotion around the farmhouse. He can see Ryan trotting between people. Tilly scurries about too, her curls streaming behind, bronze in the evening sun. She arrived this evening with her father, because her mother's at home with a baby that's not expected to live. Magnus isn't supposed to know but he overheard a conversation, and the children talk anyway. Ryan runs into the house, rushes out, sprints over to Magnus's father. Over the next minutes people put their glasses and mugs on the porch, in the flowerpots by the door, on the little tables dotted about the garden. They walk about. Talk in little knots. Spread out. Yell and shout. Magnus hears his name called over and over.

Above the noise and bustle his mother wails, her voice rising and falling like the wind around the chimney in winter. It feels unsafe, like thin ice where you could drop suddenly through a crack – like that boy two years ago they never found.

Magnus peers down through the whispering leaves, extends his foot halfway to the branch below, but it's too far, too scary to make that stretch in the deepening dusk. He looks out at the farm, thinks of waving, hollering, but his voice will be feeble against the noise below.

He should have stayed in the house, or at least the garden. But his mother was fussing about the twin cakes and Magnus didn't want two cakes, he was fed up with two cakes, and his crossness began to feel like pebbles in his stomach and a scarf tied too tight around his throat and a jitteriness in his hands and arms and chest, so he ran into the forest and climbed a tree. And he knows he should be kind and not make people sad and make them cry and now he has.

First, do no harm, says his mother every morning at breakfast: *Before anything else, first, do no harm.* Her reminder before he goes to school. He tries so hard not to hurt people, not to hurt their feelings, to be gentle and truthful and loving, all the things his mother tells him all the time. He wonders what his uncle would say. *Be kind, Magnus, she can't help it. Do no harm, Magnus.* But Magnus wouldn't have been up the tree had his uncle arrived.

Magnus shifts, easing his cramped thighs, dislodging stray fragments of leaf and bark. Something drops down his shirt. He thrashes his arms around, kicks out a leg, is millimetres away from slipping off and tumbling through the branches; gasping with fright, he works his fingers into the crevices in the bark, grips tight. Only then does he pull his shirt out from his trousers, flapping it about to let whatever landed on his skin escape. He dearly doesn't want it to be a spider – but hearing a bear would be worse. Bears climb trees.

He shoves his icy fingers into his armpits, huddles closer to the trunk, wishes he'd worn his coat and hat and scarf and gloves. His stomach empties of pebbles, and he wipes his wet eyes with his sleeve, scared of being found, scared of what will be said. Gone too long to pretend he lost track of time, maybe he'll doze off if he gets comfy and snug in his little nook, and in the morning he can climb down and run home and say, truthfully, that he fell asleep at the top of a tree.

The voices grow distant. Doors slam. Dogs bark. Torches wave around in the distant water meadows. The searchers have gone to the weir.

Magnus rummages in his pockets for something to eat but finds only a tiny, wizened apple, a stripy snail shell, two stale walnuts, seven elastic bands, a piece of string, and three almost perfectly spherical pebbles, heavy like marbles. He nibbles the hard-sour flesh of the wrinkled apple and tumbles the pebbles in his pocket, not listening to the snuffling at the base of the tree, resolutely not listening to the snapping of twigs.

Where no one has gone before

Lying half-asleep on a sloping roof of springy scented turf between two rows of solar panels, savouring the tart sweetness of midseason berries, gazing drowsily at the pale moon rising in a silver-blue sky as the soft summer frost begins to fall, you can almost believe you have landed on a foreign planet.

You and Ryan are the first astronauts ever to have seen this place, and you find the air sweet with wildflowers and hay, the birds melodious, the wooded terrain so beautiful it takes your breath away. You gather strength after your voyage, resting with half-closed eyes on this platform high above the ground, safe from marauding wild beasts, and you prepare yourselves to explore the deep and no doubt savage forest that surrounds your landing site.

Ryan reaches for more berries at the same time as you. You stare at each other, hands over the bowl. Then he laughs, his tongue stained blackberry-purple, and he shoves you, and you shove back, and he leaps on you and you push back, and you wrestle and roll together over the turf and you topple over the edge of the roof onto the hay stacked against the wall below.

Universal

Magnus and his cousin Ryan have a competition to see who can write the longest address. They think they invented this game. Magnus wins, by one line.

> Magnus of Arden,
> South-side attic bedroom,
> Oak Tree Farm,
> Meriden,
> Near Waerwic in the Forest of Arden,
> Mercia,
> Angleland,
> Islands of Breteyne,
> Europa,

Northern Sea,
Aerth,
The Solar System,
The Universe,
THE END.

Full stop.

Once upon a time

One frosty June night, long ago, an old woman woke her young son from his warm bed under the turf roof of a farmhouse in the middle of the forest. It was the boy's tenth birthday, and the stars were bright and clear. 'Get up, son,' she said. 'Come quickly!'

He followed her sleepily down the stairs to the cosy sitting room, where she wrapped him in a woollen shawl woven of all the colours of the world, and he gazed on magical images of the great explorer Niall Strong taking his first steps on Mars.

The boy's mother brought him hot milk and honey cakes for his breakfast and his father laid logs in the stove to keep him warm, for the night was chill.

When the rays of the rising sun sent their gleam through the windows and the frost patterns on the glass began to melt, the boy stretched and yawned, and said: 'Mother, I will join the explorers on Mars when I am grown.'

'No, son,' she said. 'It is too dangerous, and you are my only

child. Who will look after me if you go away? Do you not love me?'

And his father said: 'We are farmers, son. That is who we are.'

And the boy was quiet, and sorrowful, for his mother had borne nine children before him, and all had died, and he was the child of her old age, a miraculous child who had come when all seemed lost, when wolves howled in the woods and bears lifted the latches of kitchen doors and snow fell in summer, and old people placed the hope of the world in babies yet to be born.

Sometimes you have to redo your homework to make sure you've really understood it

It's not what she asked for, says his teacher. It's more fanciful than factual. Would you like to try this again?

Magnus can see her mind is already on her next student. Tilly, as it happens, who jumps around impatiently, longing to get through this and to run outside to play. His mind flicks through the hours he's meant to have written about.

> There's the summer frost, white like icing sugar; the six-day waxing moon; the grainy, blurred TV images from Mars (dull orange dust, fuzzy red mounds and boulders, the astronauts merely hazy white shapes); the

> broad, shallow buildings and tall hangars of the Space Agency, clear and crisp in the dawn light; the rows of desks and computers and the TV screen which covered an entire wall in the command centre; the serious officials.

Factual, not fanciful. He can write this, doesn't know why he didn't.

> There's his mother, her tremulous hands revealing more than celebration of an historic event. She'd promised him his tenth birthday cake shaped like the crescent moon, and it wouldn't do to upset her – it never does to upset her, ever – so he allowed her to wrap him in quilts and blankets in the overheated room, and he guzzled the honey cakes and warm milk she brought him, his hair slickening to his forehead with sweat.

Factual still. But not much good for homework. Not what his teacher would call relevant.

> There's the five astronauts descending the ladder from the spacecraft, and Magnus wriggling out of his blankets and kneeling

> on the sofa, energy surging through his muscles and nerves, his heart racing. One astronaut turned to the camera and gave a thumbs up. Niall Strong, surely, everyone's hero, although impossible to tell.

Factual, with a bit of the fanciful. Probably OK.

> There's the voice from Thetford: *And soon a colony, a town, if you will,* and Niall doing a buoyant little dance and pointing towards the horizon, then bounding away across the landscape, and the others joining him, bounding in all directions like giant bouncy toys.

Yes, she likes that kind of description. And he can mention the gravity on Mars being only 38 per cent of Aerth's, that Niall could, if he wished, jump almost three times higher than on Aerth, as long as he's been exercising properly over the months of the voyage.

> There's Magnus's heart, bounding too, and his leaping up from the sofa, his stomach a churn of excitement and ambition, the sun rising just then over the oak trees and illuminating him, his cheeks ruddy with heat and exhilaration.

Maybe?

> There's his words, unthinking, tactless: *Mother, Mother! I'll join the explorers on Mars one day!*
>
> And her reaction. *No, Magnus. No. It's too dangerous, and you're my only child. Who'll look after me when I'm old? Don't you love me?*
>
> And his father's reply: *We're farmers, son. That is who we are.*

Factual. But it doesn't put Magnus in a good light. Nor does his mother's expression – haggard, hollowed-out – or his father's anxious smile.

> There's Magnus's further lack of thought and care, perhaps deliberate, he's not sure, and right now he doesn't want to think about it: *But you're old, you'll be dead when I'm grown up, and I don't want to be a farmer!*

Definitely not.

> There's his parents' age. His mother is in in her late fifties, and looks it, wrinkled and

> grey, his father too. It's not his fault his siblings died, yet he feels the pressure and pain of it, a constant tenderness behind his breastbone, an ache behind his eyes.

These are facts, but even so.

> There's his mother's eyes, unreadable, her mouth twisted as if eating bitter herbs. There's her clattering out through the kitchen door, slamming it behind her.

All facts.

He stands before his teacher, nauseous from the memory of heat and honey cakes, feeling once more that morning's chill on his damp, sweaty skin, watching again his mother stumble across the white-frosted grass towards the wildwood, gazing still at the dark prints left by her slippered feet.

Small acts of kindness

Well of course he's sick of cake, they eat it all the time, vast quantities mounded high on the kitchen worktops, steaming from the oven, stored in every tin in the pantry: apple cake, pear cake, carrot cake, pumpkin cake; feather-light sponges; coffee or lemon or orange layer cakes; and, richest and rarest of all, dense and sticky chocolate brownies.

His father pats his waist and smiles apologetically, murmuring something about needing to watch his weight.

So it's up to Magnus to eat the cake, cake his mother makes for all his brothers' and sisters' birthdays and to remember their funeral dates…

…cake for his parents' birthdays and their wedding anniversary…

…for First Harvest (summer berries), Second Harvest (grains), Third Harvest (autumn fruits and vegetables)…

…for MidWinter, Spring Turning and Autumn Turning…

…for New Year's Eve and New Year's Day, MidSummer and every first day of the month, because, as Magnus's mother always says, it's such a blessing to have lived one more month, and how grateful we should be for a long life because many never live as long as you, my darling boy.

By the age of eleven he realises his mother staves off fear and despair and grief by making an occasion of things nobody else thinks of celebrating, like the first mushrooms in the woods or the first snowflake in autumn. He begins to suspect his mother's fragile luminous joy is as thin as the first ice on the lake in September, ice that melts by breakfast time and wouldn't hold a sparrow.

He develops strategies for getting rid of the cake: he invites friends to tea; he takes whole cakes to share at school; he slips cake into the chickens' mash.

One morning he takes a shortcut to school, a narrow animal path deep in the woods where his mother never walks, a path all children are forbidden to tread. Under the bronzing leaves of the tallest oak, Magnus unwraps his slice of lunch-time walnut cake and crumbles it into the undergrowth for the birds. Behind him something snaps, like brittle twigs. Magnus straightens, casually picks up his bag and saunters on, not looking back, as the forest crackles and breathes behind him.

Where the truth lies

For homework this weekend Magnus must interview a family member who lived through the crisis of the second great wave. He'll be interviewing his mother, because his father has gone away to buy a horse.

Magnus wishes he'd never heard of the wave. He wishes people had been kind enough to keep him in ignorance, but apparently everyone needs to know, because those who forget the past (*I never forgot anything, I never knew about it!*) are condemned to repeat it. Now Magnus is twelve the wave turns up in every subject in school. History, geography, ethics, literature, philosophy, science, maths, art, farming… it influences everything, taints everything, provides nothing worth remembering in this life where he is always, always, being told to be kind and truthful and loving and considerate. Magnus fails to see exactly what he's supposed to learn from this litany of disaster.

It's disgusting, nightmarish – deformed babies, lingering

deaths, loss of reason and memory, withering of limbs, blindness, incontinence – and Magnus does have nightmares, dreams from which he wakes screaming, dreams in which his eyes fall out and his fingers drop off one by one, and in which his mother doesn't notice his growing distress but tells him to eat his greens, go feed the chickens and learn his times tables. He's grown up with too many stories to take the wave as lightly as his classmates, maybe because his parents are old, as old as his friends' grandparents, and they haven't much else to talk about. At least, his mother does the talking, and his father reads a book.

He watches his mother furtively, waiting for the right opportunity to approach her, when she's not busy or tired or irritated. He's not observed her before, not in this way, not when he's leading up to something so momentous; he's not noticed how distracted she appears, how she mutters about government this, government that, *doing no bloody harm.* Magnus wonders whether she's always done this and how it is he can live with someone and not hear her.

Magnus asks her about his status, and she replies sharply, indignantly, that she should know, she had nine who didn't make it.

'You don't need testing, Magnus. Take it from me. You wouldn't be here if you carried the virus.' She breaks off, turns abruptly away, grabs the chickens' food pail and marches outside.

Magnus's interview, entirely imaginary, is awarded an A star and a commendation for its sensitivity.

Aching with tension, Magnus doesn't hurry, although every nerve screams that he should run. He reaches into his bag, takes his slice of cloth-wrapped fruitcake and tosses it onto the path, which is barely a path, now he looks at it, now his senses are heightened by the unexpectedness of this encounter, by the proximity to this animal, by his knowledge that he has no idea what it might do, that he's very far from help if things get dangerous.

The path, he sees in about half a second, is by no means a path, and yes, he did know this, but recently he has enjoyed pushing his way through the shrubby understorey, making his way from clearing to clearing, pretending he is an explorer on a new world.

The path, it's true to say, is more a kind of animal track, the kind of track that small creatures make, suitable neither for humans nor for the larger mammal; and now he recognises where branches have been snapped off and brambles trampled by something big.

Magnus has never until today seen evidence of bears. He decided years ago that stories of wolves and bears were folk tales invented to scare young children around winter hearths. Yet a brown bear snuffles the dust exactly where Magnus has been scattering cake for the birds. It takes quick, sharp breaths, its nostrils quiver, the brown fur on its flanks trembles. Dry bits of leaf lift and drop on the narrow path as if blown by a gentle breeze. The bear is four times Magnus's size.

The left side of its face is streaked white, almost luminous in the half-light of the forest.

The bear lifts its head and stares at him, a long, unblinking stare, then snorts as it sniffs the air, moving its head from side to side as if to ascertain whether Magnus is real. It moves one foot forward.

Magnus takes a step back, then stops, his palms pricking with sweat. What is it you're supposed to do? Move? Not move? Play dead?

Between them lies the cake, half-wrapped in a square from one of Magnus's father's old shirts. It's dark and rich and it glistens. Magnus can smell it from here, the raisins and the brandy and the butter and the golden honey. He can smell the bear too, acrid, musky, loamy, forest-y.

The bear lowers its head and sniffs the cake. Magnus cautiously takes one step back, then another, and another, until he's out of view behind a clump of hazel bushes. Twigs and things crack beneath his feet. He doesn't look down to see, holds his breath, doesn't move, listens. His heart thumps, loud and urgent, and he tries to quieten his breathing. For a brief moment he's cross – why did nobody ever tell him about the bears? Although perhaps they did, but there's no time to think about that right now.

He can hear snuffling, and a kind of slobbery sound as if the bear's drooling and licking. Well of course it likes cake, all that honey and fruit. Bears like honey and fruit. Everyone knows that.

Magnus turns, hurtles down the slope to the wooden

fence at the edge of the trees, clambers over the stile and races through the meadows, startling birds which rise with calls of alarm from the long grasses and reeds; he leaps tussocks, weaving around the cows which loom out of the mist and stare at him impassively, their breath in clouds; and he careens up the lane to the Moot Hall, bursting through the heavy oak doors which crash behind him against the soft white plaster walls, and is thirty-five minutes late for school, with no excuse or reason good enough, because, as everyone knows, children are forbidden to take shortcuts through the woods.

First, do no harm (1)

'You can spend a lifetime thinking about this,' says Hilden.

Magnus smiles politely. *A lifetime? Seriously?* He turns his gaze to the glowing embers of the log fire. The house is dim and smoky, but warm. It smells of cat piss. Hilden's incontinent cat keeps out the mice, she told him when he walked through the door, trying not to wrinkle his nose at the smell, trying to be as tactful and attentive as possible to this woman chosen by his parents to guide him through the – apparently turbulent – years ahead. The incontinent cat and the smell seemed excellent reasons for refusing tea.

Hilden offered him tea when he arrived, but Magnus said he wasn't thirsty, which wasn't true. Now he wishes he'd accepted. It'd give him something to do with his hands, something to look at rather than Hilden's wrinkly face, her wispy white hair pinned back in a straggle, and her dark brown eyes, those unnerving eyes which seem to know him, even though they've met for the first time this afternoon. It'd be rude to stare at her books, gaze out of the window, peer at her wood carvings. Next time he'll say yes to tea.

'*First*, do no harm. First, do no *harm*. First, do *no* harm. *First, do no harm.*'

She has a gentle voice, soothing and melodious, despite being old. Magnus associates oldness with toughness. Every other old person in the village – his mother, for example – is tough, stern, humourless. Life's not easy, he gets that: eight months of winter and a brief spring, followed by a few chilly weeks of summer to grow enough food to store for the year.

He wonders how Ryan's getting on with his own mentor. Thursdays, after school, no excuses. All twelve-year-olds begin their mentoring today. *Ugh.*

Hilden asks questions about the cat: 'Which is less harmful? The cat dribbling urine around the house? Or mice eating winter stores, dribbling their own urine over food in the storeroom and kitchen? Dropping their pellets?'

Magnus doesn't reply. He doesn't know the right answer, so he'll just think about things. It's not like school. Or home. It's not like anything. *Six years of this. Six years.*

Hilden continues: 'Is disease from contaminated food more harmful than discomfort suffered by the human nose?'

Who knows? The smell's sickening. Six years. Week after week. I'll be eighteen!

'If I get another cat, will that be harmful to my current cat? She's not sick enough to be put down. Or put to sleep. Whichever euphemism you prefer.'

What's a euphemism?

'What about killing animals that have outlived their usefulness, Magnus? Or sick humans?'

Don't like the idea of killing humans. Except Ryan. Magnus suppresses a smirk.

Hilden puts another log on the fire.

'You're learning how to think, Magnus.'

I know how to think. I'm thinking right now. I'm thinking you're a stupid old woman and I want to go home.

This is how you learn to fly

It's a trek, the annual school trip to the museum in Town. Four miles on footpaths through the forest, with adults carrying shotguns or rifles, *just in case*. Nobody spells out exactly what kind of emergency would need weapons, although Magnus has a fairly good idea. This little jaunt encroaches on the territory of large wild animals, so the smallest children, those under seven – precious few of them these days – stay behind in the care of whoever can spare the time. Everyone else ambles along and gets to Town eventually.

As they walk it begins to snow, dry picture-book flakes in pretty six-sided shapes that linger on sleeves and shoulders.

It's the best kind of snowy weather; the air so keen it almost freezes your breath, so dry that your hair stands up with static when you take off your hat. Everyone is perfectly warm, walking along. Not like that heavy westerly snow that makes your clothes soggy and you chilled through.

In the museum Magnus makes immediately for the huge rotating globe, his favourite display. It turns slowly under the light of the lamp which represents the Sun. He sweeps his fingers over bumpy grey mountain ranges: the Pennines, the Grampians, Snowdonia, all the wrong colour. They should be white because of their year-round snow. Mountainous Italia and Nippon are almost entirely grey, with thin strips of green along the coastlines. And the Norse lands should be surrounded by white sea ice, not blue ocean.

So, the globe is out of date, but it's still his favourite, and anyone who thinks it's stupid is an idiot. He glances up at the lamp, shining on northern Europa. He'd love to work out a way of making the lamp shine most on the equator, which, as everyone knows, is the place to be. Given the chance, he'd travel somewhere hot, go barefoot, take off his jumpers, feel the warmth of sun on his skin. Only a handful of times in his thirteen years has the air ever been mild enough that school closed for the day in celebration, and adults abandoned their work, and they picnicked together by the river.

Today's homework is to write an imaginative excursion to a part of the world he's never seen and, it goes without saying, is never likely to: five hundred words, to be handed in on Monday morning.

It's impossible to imagine what he's never experienced, although his teacher says that's nonsense. People make up stories all the time, she says. What about dragons?

She's old; it's easy for her. She's done things he'll never get to do. She travelled to Italia when she was young and picked grapes – she can imagine loads! Magnus can't. In his imagination he wears a coat in summer, hat and gloves stuffed in pockets for when the clouds come over; in his imagination he carries a hot dinner in an insulated container; in his imagination he's rolling up his trousers to play in the stream when hail or sleet stings his bare head and he runs for cover.

Magnus gazes at those magnificent twin inland seas, the North and South Mediterraneans, and feels a stir of desperation. He traces the outlines of Italia and Hellas and Spania; the islands of Algeria and Libya; the island-continent of Maroc. As the globe turns, he brushes his fingertips over the powdered moss-green flock representing forest, that wild and ancient woodland which covers by far the greater part of Aerth's land masses, and he settles on the astounding Ring of Australis, with its enormous central freshwater lake.

His teacher is talking about the essay assignment, but he doesn't hear her. He's watching the globe, caressing its lands and seas, his ears deafened by the howling, wailing, roaring, hissing, screeching, singing forests of the Aerth.

How things are done

No, they said, you're too young to stay home alone. What with the bear. Or bears.

Magnus sits, bored, at the back of the medieval Moot Hall while the discussion grinds on. There are no other young people here, they've all been allowed to stay home, although, now he looks, not all the parents have attended this meeting. It's mostly the mothers.

The evidence: an orchard gate smashed, barrels of apples upturned, hives prised open and the honey gone. Magnus wonders how badly the bear was stung, or if the bees couldn't sting because of the bear's thick coat. He imagines it sitting on its backside in the middle of the orchard, licking its paws, its claws and muzzle sticky with golden apple-blossom honey. Or triumphantly carrying off the honeycombs in its jaws.

He fiddles with his shoelaces. He has brought homework but is distracted by tiredness and overfamiliarity, since the Moot Hall is his schoolroom four days a week: ancient black oak pillars, and branches half-embedded in the walls, whitewashed spaces between them – triangles but not quite, rectangles and squares but not quite. Magnus once ruined a penknife on the oak beam nearest his seat. Seasoned oak-wood, he learned that day, is tough, dense, solid, does not easily yield.

Markets are held here in winter. Weddings, funerals, town planning. It all happens here. He argued over supper that he'd be safe at home, but bears have been known to lift latches and enter houses in search of food. Nobody, said his mother, wants to start locking their houses. And nobody would leave their only child in danger. Certainly not her. Magnus knows exactly what she means, and he can't argue with that.

The familiar arguments against violence ring out. The tenor of the meeting is becoming as heated as it's ever going to in a community that espouses pacifism and believes that talking can solve all problems, and Magnus is bored, *bored, bored!* Violence can never be justified, say the elders, Magnus's parents among them, however compelling the need for violence may appear. How shall we persuade the bears to depart? How might we dissuade them from seeking easy pickings, if this coming winter turns out even harsher than the last? When should a rifle or shotgun be permitted? *First, do no harm… Walk gently on the Aerth.*

Magnus turns to the wildlife book in his satchel, skims the pages until he reaches the section on bears: Because of the changing climate, bears are moving south, becoming more numerous as summer contracts and winter lengthens year by year, as snow lasts till May and begins again in September, as drifts lie deeper each year around the houses and the farms. Bears like fruit and honey and fish, berries and vegetables and eggs. They eat small mammals, too, and they'll always attack to protect their young.

What you must never, ever do is feed a bear.

Magnus stares a long time at this page, before quietly closing the book and putting it away alongside the wrapped slice of apple cake his mother has given him in case he gets hungry, alongside the memory of crumbs scattered in the woods.

New lands for old

On the coldest afternoons in deepest winter, when chores are done and homework completed, when snow falls so thick and fast that even the three of them working together can't keep up with clearing the path from house to barn, Magnus lies on his front on the home-woven brown and cream wool rug in the sitting room, intent on continents, islands, ice, desert, forests and oceans.

The oldest atlas was bought by his great-great-great-something grandparents over four hundred years ago. Brittle and frayed with age, the pages show puffed faces blowing wind through pursed lips, whales riding curling waves, dragons straddling needle-like mountains. Tiny giraffes gallop over ochre deserts. Miniature pagodas rise from the centres of even tinier cities. Countries coloured in the palest pink or blue or green or yellow are riven by azure rivers, encircled by emerald forests. When Magnus was little he thought the ground itself must be pink or blue or green or yellow, that people dressed in the colours of their lands, that their homes were painted in those pastels, like illustrations in books of nursery rhymes.

A photographic atlas of Mars is the most recent, a gift last year from Magnus's uncle to his father. Mars is dusty red, scattered with rust-coloured rocks under a salmon-pink sky, its clouds streaked tangerine and scarlet, the ice caps of its North and South Poles growing and receding according to the season. The centre of the book holds images and diagrams of New Thetford, the colony established by Niall Strong, where hundreds of physicists, atmospheric chemists, botanists, microbiologists, medical doctors and agronomists have made their home. Bored by the lists of names and disciplines Magnus turns the pages quickly, hungry for more pictures, landing at last on the geodesic farming domes with their bright green crops visible through transparent walls, their curving roofs gleaming in the pale sunlight. Alongside the domes, the living quarters and scientific labs are small and insignificant. Without food there's no life, after all. Everyone knows that.

Magnus peers at the all-terrain vehicles parked neatly in rows nearby: large, small, four- or six- or eight-wheeled, caterpillar-tracked, articulated; some used for week-long expeditions, others for local trips. He reads avidly the specifications for each vehicle: two or twenty people, the capacity for supplies, water, extra oxygen, samples of rock and dirt, first aid equipment, short-wave radios, spare uniforms, food. He thinks, briefly, of the machine dump at the edge of his village, out of bounds to all but a few and certainly forbidden to children. From the top of his favourite tree he's able to see a battered yellow scoop, a rusted red trailer, three huge worn tyres; but until he's eighteen these details are all he'll have, and how they fit together will remain frustratingly mysterious.

Behind the Martian agridomes, ankle-high forests of tough little conifers run up the shallow slopes of a long hill. Their roots already anchor the soil, their needle-leaves already create tiny amounts of oxygen, and one day they'll encourage precipitation. They look like black ants against the red earth.

It's pioneering work, inspiring, a brilliant visionary exercise in bringing a dead planet back to life; or it's a waste of effort and time, all – according to Magnus's mother – a crying in the wind of extinction. He's not entirely sure what she means, but this is the book he smuggles upstairs under his dressing gown to read in bed by torchlight.

Midnight feast

Magnus switches off the torch and navigates by the yellow harvest moon rising over the towering oaks. Above, the Milky Way turns slowly, luminous in the blue-black sky. The galaxy is a collection of hills and valleys, the moon a wheel of cheese about to be rolled down the slopes by sky giants. Over the solid frozen ground the air is so cold and clean that sounds travel far, clear and crisp: an owl, a dog barking, the sharp crack of a branch succumbing to the bitter frost. No snow yet, it's only mid September. The first fall of fresh snow is always exciting, and Magnus never tires of it, but for eight months a year he snowshoes two miles each way to school, and deep snow has lost its glamour.

He approaches the shed warily, staring at the dark oblong where the door should be, wondering who left it open. His foot kicks against something small and round which trickles away and bumps softly into other small round things. They settle against each other a few feet from the doorway, rocking gently. Onions. He turns on his torch.

A huge bear sprawls over the jute sacks containing their winter supplies: carrots, parsnips, beets, onions, hard white cabbages. Its eyelids are swollen and fused together with dried mucus, its muzzle bumpy with lumps and swollen scratches, the fur on its face crusted with dried blood. The bear turns its head blindly towards him, snuffling the air, and gives a little grunt. Magnus knows this bear; he recognises the distinctive white blaze on its cheek, for a few seconds experiences again his terror the day they met in the woods, when it licked up with its great drooling tongue the crumbs of cake he'd been scattering for the birds. He tenses, ready to run, his breathing quick and shallow, but understands almost immediately that the bear is uncertain and afraid, and he stays where he is.

Bees, it has to be. Against the pain and itching of the stings the bear has gouged its own muzzle with its great claws. This is the bear (or one of the bears) that's been ripping open the hives in orchards. This is the bear that has learned to forage from human habitation. This is the bear that's striking fear and conflict deep into the hearts of people across four villages.

This is the bear nobody wants to kill.

Magnus switches off his light and steps backwards out of the shed. Silently he closes the door and drops the latch before the bear has a chance to move. Then he stands perfectly still, waiting to hear from his heart what he should do.

First, do no harm (2)

'What would happen if a person is found to be feeding bears?'

Hilden turns from pouring tea. 'Bears?'

'Or wolves. Or other dangerous animals. Lynxes, maybe.'

'First do no harm, Magnus.'

'I know. So, what would happen?'

'We should take a number of things into consideration, not least harm done to the animal.'

'The animal?'

'If animals learn that humans are good sources of food, and teach their young to forage among human habitation, wouldn't you say harm has been done?'

Magnus shrugs.

'If animals eat unsuitable food, their health suffers. They weaken. Their senses become less acute. They take the lazy option. What if it's winter and there are no fruits in the orchards, no grain in the fields, no berries in the hedgerows? If the hens are locked away?'

'They starve?'

'Perhaps. Or they may crave tasty morsels from human kitchens. They may decide to break in.'

Magnus leans forward to do up his shoelace, which he has just this minute noticed isn't tight enough.

'What if a householder discovers a bear in her kitchen and to protect her family reaches for a gun? Shoots the bear? What if the bear has young?'

Magnus looks everywhere except into Hilden's eyes. He examines his mug of tea (stoneware, blue and white), the cuffs of his brown corduroy trousers (a bit muddy but not damp), the crocheted blanket on Hilden's battered old sofa (her daughter made it not long before she died), and he stays with this blanket, analysing the complexity of the coloured patterns, the reds and greens and russets, the colours of the forest in autumn, and avoids looking at Hilden, who is sitting at the far end of the sofa, half the blanket on her lap.

'I imagine the cubs may starve to death, Magnus.'

Magnus gives the tiniest nod.

'The householder, Magnus. Let's think about her. She may be devastated at the unnecessary slaughter of a wild animal that is merely trying to feed its young. She'll have the words *First do no harm* ringing in her ears, as they no doubt are beginning to ring in yours after this past year's instruction. Has harm been done to this woman, Magnus?'

Magnus shakes his head.

'You think not?'

Magnus clears his throat. 'I mean, I don't know.'

'You can think about it for homework this week.'

Magnus looks up. 'You don't give me homework.'

'It's at my discretion. Now, shall we think about wolves?'

No secrets

When Magnus's mother speaks, everyone listens. 'Everyone' means Magnus and his father.

'I don't understand this government obsession with colonising Mars.'

She makes this statement weekly, at least.

Magnus looks at his plate. He's finished dinner, is waiting for tonight's cake. His mother has recently stopped making desserts, for which he's thankful. Cake is enough.

She clatters her spoon inside her mug, stirring the dregs of her tea. 'It's not as if we don't have enough problems here, without starting again on another planet. It's not as if Mars is habitable.'

'They'll have their reasons,' says Magnus's father peaceably. Magnus darts him a look. Of course they've got reasons. It wouldn't make sense otherwise.

'Why young single adults? Why the secrecy?' She stands abruptly, gathering plates and knives with quick, impatient movements. Her chair teeters for a few seconds on its back legs, then crashes onto the stone floor. 'There are no secrets, apparently,' she adds, bitterly. 'Everything's open and transparent, so they say.'

'Does it matter to us, here in Arden?' His father stands. He picks up the chair, puts his arm around his wife's shoulder and pulls her close.

She shrugs him off, continues, her voice harsh. 'We've never been given any proper explanation. I thought we'd passed the age of secrets.'

Magnus can feel her anxiety, but that's constant, it spikes up and down daily, more up than down. His father, he can't be sure, but he seems… bored…?

Magnus's heart, though, oh man, it's racing, pounding, thundering in his chest. He keeps his eyes down, sits still, hopes the pulse in his neck isn't visible. A voice in his head shouts: *I want I want I want… Mars… Mars… Mars…*

'Sweetheart, I see no harm.'

'I should have gone into leadership when I had the chance.' She pulls away, her body stiff and unyielding, walks to the sink and drops all the plates and cutlery into the bowl. Something cracks.

There must be good reasons to colonise Mars… I want… if I got there, I'd show her… I'd show everyone… they'd be so proud…

His father glances at him.

How can he? Can he? Can Dad hear me? At fifteen, there are enough mysteries in life that telepathy, right now, doesn't seem unlikely.

His father winks.

Magnus takes the hint, the only thing possible in the circumstances.

'Mmm, cake?'

'Well, it's obvious. *Listen with all your heart* means listening carefully. Or observing what people are feeling, through their body language.'

'That's a good start.'

'Oh.'

Magnus has thought about this for days, examining it from different angles, listening compassionately, seeing situations from other people's points of view. He does this with his mother, in any case. It's almost like that's all she ever says: *See it from my point of view, Magnus, for once. Put yourself in my shoes for a change.*

'What else, Magnus?'

'I've no idea.'

'But you do.' Hilden touches both her ears with her forefingers. 'Listen.'

They're walking at the edge of the forest on almost the last clear afternoon before the snow comes. Magnus scuffs dead leaves with his boots, trying to pay attention with his ears: the wind sighing so quietly in the oaks that at first he misses it; tiny animals scurrying in the undergrowth; children at play; the solid beat of his heart; his breathing, regular and irregular as he walks and climbs.

'Total immersion, like being underwater,' she adds.

He can't imagine anything worse. She clearly doesn't mean a bath. Maybe when she was young the weather was warm enough to swim outside.

He hears farther off the rush of the river over the weir, the clank and jingle of a horse's harness, the creak of cart wheels. He begins to hear internal voices: his mother's, reminding him to hurry home for supper; his own – has he practised enough for tonight's concert? – Ryan's, telling him the latest news from Mars. And far away, like a rustling in the forest, a heart-whisper of hope that Tilly may smile at him tonight.

In comparison, *Walking gently* is easy, and he said so last week. It's about being kind. But now he suspects that walking gently may be as complicated as doing no harm and listening with all your heart, which seems to mean your entire heart, head, body, mind and everything else besides.

He'll never be wise enough, good enough. Or even enough.

'Don't imagine that moral instruction is about attaining perfection, Magnus.'

'But that's what it seems. Don't harm, listen, be gentle, live truth, love. That's being perfect, isn't it?'

'This side of heaven none of us is capable of perfection, Magnus.'

Magnus stares at his mentor in disbelief. From early childhood he's been taught that this is all that exists. There's no afterlife, no spiritual salvation beyond the grave. No heaven. Just Aerth. *Humans have made their beds and they must lie in them.*

'We don't believe in heaven,' he says at last. 'We believe in heaven on Aerth.'

Hilden smiles. 'Well, my dear. Now we're getting somewhere.'

'This Space Agency application, Magnus.' The magistrate gives an almost imperceptible sigh. 'Is this course of action useful and necessary? Could it be harmful? Have you been listening with all your heart?'

Magnus boils with indignation. Sweat trickles from his armpits and down his back, soaking his undershirt. The gold letters carved into the black oak beam over the head of the magistrate mock him: FIRST, DO NO HARM. A permanent state of fury's surely more harmful than the alternative, that of knuckling down and doing what everyone else decides for him.

'I'm seventeen! I'm old enough to know my own mind, and for heart's sake I've known my path for years, I've always known. It's ridiculous it's even come to this!' He glares at the magistrate. 'I tell you, it's necessary for my well-being. It'll kill me if I don't do this. I'll go mad with grief.'

The magistrate gazes at him, her face unreadable. Magnus feels his argument is carrying less weight than it should. It sounded all right in his bedroom.

He takes a breath, tries to seem calm. 'It's to the benefit of the whole world, furthering knowledge. What harm could it do?'

'The harm may be to your parents' well-being, Magnus. Possibly their health too. You are their only surviving child, after all.'

Magnus holds her gaze. He knows the truth of this. He could back out right now, and no more would be said, but he can be stubborn when he chooses, he's been told this often enough, and today he chooses.

The magistrate shakes her head in a tiny movement that conveys more than exasperation – disappointment, perhaps, or sorrow.

'Furthermore, Magnus, necessity is a wide term and may, therefore, be applied widely. It's not necessary to our community that you study at the Space Agency. However, it is necessary that you remain here, as a young, healthy adult. We cannot give you our blessing or support.' She peers at Magnus over the top of her glasses. 'We have to balance, as you know full well, individual needs, wants and aspirations against the needs of the community.' She shuffles the papers in front of her. 'You may do as you see fit, Magnus, when you're eighteen. We trust you will meditate upon the possible outcomes of hasty action.'

Magnus's heart pounds and his ears ring with the thud of his pulse. Nobody's been listening to him, nobody at all. He speaks quietly, but his voice trembles, his whole body trembles.

'My parents' well-being is their own business. They're pretty tough. They'll survive.'

There's a collective intake of breath around the room. Magnus picks up his coat and scarf and hat and strides over the wide polished floorboards to the double oak doors at the back of the medieval Moot Hall.

'Magnus. We've not finished discussing this matter.'

He spins round, breathless with outrage, staring at the magistrate, this middle-aged woman who taught him in kindergarten. He remembers the modest comforts of that time: the achievement of learning his letters, plasters on his grazed knees, the bitter scent of wax crayons, the hunt for tiny creatures on nature walks, his teacher's faint perfume of lavender.

'I've finished.'

He turns and with both hands pushes hard against the heavy carved doors. They swing back with a satisfying thud, the handles gouging deep, jagged holes in the soft walls. Chunks of plaster drop like hailstones onto the tiles as he steps into the freezing fog.

Alternative arrangements

On the evening of his eighteenth birthday, Magnus smiles at the faces turned in greeting as he enters the Moot Hall behind his father and sits beside Tilly, who beams at him. They've graduated from school to this simple evening college, where after a full day's work they will come four nights a week, take notes, learn how to provide food for the long cold season when the soft fertile soil becomes hard as rock, nine months of the year. Eight months, if they're lucky. Glaciers are advancing from the north, and one day this land, these farms, will no longer be viable, and everyone will have left. But for now, they stay.

As they leave the hall, Tilly and Magnus hold hands, fingers entwined. Magnus has given her a ring made of thread-thin twisted willow which she wears on the third finger of her left hand. They push their way through the knee-deep snow, and they kiss behind Tilly's parents' cowshed, pushing their cold hands under each other's clothes, warming them against each other's bare skin, their hot breath mingling in clouds.

They have aspirations, too, and make fantastical plans of travelling south, to warmth and sun. No one they know has ever done this, but why shouldn't they? It's not so outlandish. Centuries ago people travelled, wrote books, made drawings and paintings and photographs, brought home plants and seeds, art and music. Tilly longs to visit Italia, to eat fresh grapes straight from the vine, to sail the North and South Mediterraneans and climb the mountains of Maroc. Magnus yearns for the singing forests of the Guarani. They can do both! Why not! They'll come back one day, have children and settle, but not yet, not yet.

Over his first adult winter Magnus quietly shelves his ambitions to go into space. Instead he drifts to sleep each night with his mind full of Tilly: her wildly curly hair, her soft mouth, her blue eyes sparkling like stars in a winter sky, her freckles scattered like the Milky Way.

Seismic

Pregnancy takes Magnus and Tilly by surprise, although at eighteen it really shouldn't. They know the facts of life. But their baby boy is born too early, a tiny child no bigger than a kitten. Magnus runs home, fresh from weeping at Tilly's bedside, and bursts into a kitchen full of people: his parents, their siblings, their oldest friends.

He marches from stove to table, table to door, clutching his head. He'd been so excited at being a father, had assumed his child would be healthy, like him and Tilly. He feels let down, not only by his dreams but by the generation before.

Magnus hardens his heart at his mother's tear-stained face. 'You said I didn't need testing. You said you had nine who didn't make it. You said you'd know if I was sick. So, tell me, what does that mean? Am I a carrier? Is Tilly? Are you?'

She shakes her head, remains silent. These are unfair questions and he knows it. Magnus jabs his finger at his mother's friend, the magistrate, his former kindergarten teacher.

'You say the virus is wearing itself out, but I don't believe you! You know more than you say. You hide the truth. Tell me – tell all of us – how can we live well if we don't know the truth?'

He swings round and grasps his mother's arm, shakes her so hard that she looks like a floppy doll.

'Do you want us to end up like this? Insane with grief? Living in the past, scared of the future?'

His mother pulls away, her eyes wide, fearful. Magnus is briefly ashamed, but then remembers everything that hurts: birthdays that revolve around dead people… his mother's incessant cake-baking… being dissuaded from a career he'd love… his parents' forensic focus on him, their future… the lifestyle, the belief system, in which everyone else comes first.

What about him, his needs, his wants? His anger surges like a volcano, heat rising to his skin, his limbs shaking with suppressed energy.

His father steps towards him but Magnus is quicker; he drops his mother's arm, lunges forward, shoves him away. His father falls back, sprawls across the table, arms splayed, white hair straggling over the bread and butter, the iced coffee cake crushed. Cups and plates shatter on the stone floor.

Magnus grabs the nearest chair, raises it above his head to fling it across the room at the group of people huddled by the big old armchair, worn and faded, a place of comfort and love where as a small child he curled up with his mother or father, reading books and telling stories, a place where the cats sleep, a place of safety.

He stops, his arms raised, immobile, suddenly appalled. He sees himself as if from afar, his violence a shock he feels in his guts. He's never hit anyone in his life; he never imagined he was capable of such cruelty, such hatred. His parents' only crime is to have given him life, loved and nurtured him, protected him from danger, from his own self. It's not their fault they're old.

Magnus begins to shake, his anger abruptly quenched by shame. Someone takes the chair gently from him.

His father has been helped up and now bends to the broken crockery. Tears fill Magnus's eyes in pity and self-pity. Every person he knows has experienced similar griefs, many times. He stands alone in the centre of the room, not daring to look up, not daring to see what may be in people's eyes.

Going south

Tilly flings open her window and tells him breathlessly, astonishingly, that she's travelling next month to cousins at Winchcombe. They invited her ages ago, before the baby, and why not now, after all?

Her excitement is palpable, her eyes wide, her lips curving on the edge of a smile. She's always wanted to travel – and what an adventure! – fifty miles on horseback through the wildwood. And then the city, the capital!

Magnus can't breathe, can't catch his breath for excitement, for the sense that the world is finally opening up to him. 'Then we can travel, like we always planned! We can go anywhere!'

He thinks of Wessex in the south: fertile land, a milder climate, friendly people; they're desperate for new blood, for young energy; they're giving farms away, free, gratis! And won't it be great to start afresh, no history! They can have more babies, healthy, happy babies, they can buck the trend!

Before he can say any of this, Tilly says: 'Oh, but I'm going on my own.'

New ground

Before dawn on his twenty-first birthday Magnus packs his rucksack with a change of clothes and his toothbrush, and creeps downstairs. In the letter he places under the teapot he doesn't apologise for leaving today, on his birthday, but tells his parents he has accepted the Space Agency's offer of training. It's brief, a scrawl of a few lines, but he does at least say he loves them. The dogs raise their heads and thump their tails sleepily as he wraps bread and cheese and a few dried apple slices in a cloth. He lifts the door latch and steps into the crisp air.

It's close to the summer solstice, and is light before four. A frost lingers on the long grass by the side of the old high road, once so wide you could have put houses on it, now narrow and crowded with elms, ash, holly, rowan and saplings of birch and larch and oak, and a dense understorey that has broken through the hard surface. Despite the chill Magnus becomes hot within minutes in his woollen clothing. His breath comes in thick clouds, his cheeks sting, but he slips off his outer garments and straps them to his bag.

A mile out of Meriden, past the machine dump, past the carp lake, where the forest begins to thicken and darken, he stops at the graveyard. Venerable lichen-splodged stones with illegible names lean sideways as if hit by a minor earthquake. Generations of ancestors are buried here. His nine siblings lie further on, with almost all his cousins, and the brothers and sisters of his friends. Their simple oak markers stretch for acres through land cleared of the wildwood: oaks and beeches and elms and ash felled, brambles and hazel grubbed out by men like his father and grandfather, men who sweated and groaned and injured themselves, and, yes, who even died on this hallowed ground. Their huge horses dragged giant trees out of the forest every summer, year after year after year, clearing the ground for the dead.

Magnus considers going in and laying a leafy twig on the place where each of his siblings lies.

But… if he walks into that memorial ground, if he spends time honouring siblings he never knew, honouring his mother's grief, honouring the losses sustained now by three generations… the truth is it's entirely possible, if not probable, that he'll turn back, arrive home in time for breakfast and never leave Meriden again.

Hosteller

✦ *The word 'Host' is related to Hostel, hotel, hospital, hospice, hospitable and hospitality.*

✦ *After long experience it has become apparent that it is better not to separate these functions.*

✦ *Guests are requested to introduce themselves to the Host on arrival. All contribute to the life of the community.*

✦ *Welcome, guest.*

His room is small and white, its tiny window overlooking the narrow road. Sleep is elusive. His conversation with the Host rings in his heart while he dozes; the bright moon wakes him fully around midnight. By dawn he stands by the open curtain, watching the nightlife as it turns to daylife. Two wolves slink into the trees, a trio of fox cubs tumble on the gravel, owls of varying sizes swoop overhead, bats flutter. What he mistook for a large rock partly hidden by scrub rises and ambles off. An elk.

As the light turns from dark grey to light grey to gold, birds begin to sing, a deafening chorus designed to wake the world. A red squirrel lands on a branch, its tail quivering. Human voices call, greet each other, issue instructions. Clanking drifts through the open kitchen windows and doors.

The Host was busy when he arrived yesterday evening – a medical emergency – but she sought him out after supper. She reminds him uncomfortably of his mentor Hilden. Something about the eyes, that steady gaze that seeks out the hidden parts of a person's soul.

They spoke of his onward journey, how many days' walking, how many Hostel visits. She suggested he should stay at each Hostel for a minimum of three nights, as a form of meditation, a time for reflection, an opportunity to assess whether his intentions are true. She reminded him, in passing, that the word *guest* is related to *host*, both words from the same ancient root. *Guests and hosts have reciprocal responsibilities*, she said, and smiled.

Magnus stands by his window and works it out again. Hostels are five miles apart. Twenty-two Hostels. Two months, at least. Not that the Host's suggestions are conditions, but like Hilden's they are always wiser than his own ideas. Are they in touch with each other, the Hosts? Do they warn each other of difficult characters? Do they have the power to turn him back?

In the dining room breakfast is served at the long counter by a bald woman with a canula in the back of her hand. A teenage lad, his face, neck and arms scarred by burns, moves slowly between the tables, collecting dishes. The older man sitting opposite Magnus, a male mentor (how unusual, and how unfortunate for Magnus) thanks Magnus for such an informative conversation about the complexities of wild camping, and says he's off to do a spot of gardening. Magnus can smell the freshly mown grass from here. They glance together through the open doors into the central garden, where pots of herbs are tucked into beds of hollyhocks, and on the far side, under a veranda entwined with pale roses and honeysuckle, two young men push a child on a wheeled bed towards five people tuning musical instruments.

Magnus collects a mop and bucket to wash the stairs. He'll stay a night or two, think over his options. Call his parents. Say sorry for running away. Think about *hostile* and *hostage*, words nobody uses these days.

Heart whispering

In Magnus's third week at the Space Agency, new information comes his way in the form of a most astonishing lecture: an Aerth-like planet has been discovered circling the Sun at the same distance from the Sun as Aerth itself; it is, in fact, concealed by the Sun. *Aerth Two*, or, as the other planet calls itself, *Urth*.

How these twin planets have arisen is unknown. Some say that one planet has made an incursion into the other's universe. Others talk about a mirrorverse and dark matter. All Magnus knows is that he'd do anything to be part of any team that visits Urth.

It seems Urth can't afford to send astronauts to Aerth, or perhaps their technology isn't advanced enough. It's not quite clear. So a team of Aerth's brightest and healthiest astronauts will travel to Mars, and from there to Urth. It'll take time, but these things can't – shouldn't – be hurried.

Magnus takes the three almost perfectly spherical pebbles he keeps in his pocket – blue-green, red and brown – and considers his options. How to quote his professor without quoting her directly. How to indicate, without stating it baldly, that he, Magnus, would be an ideal candidate for expeditions to other planets. How to convey most clearly, without ambiguity or overstating his case, that he is, himself, immune from homesickness and grief, and he tumbles the pebbles in his fingers.

His imagination gallops ahead. He imagines he's chosen, accepts, makes the call he dreads; he imagines his mother stumbling out of the house, clambering through the wildwood under the ancient oaks, pushing aside brambles and ferns, startling deer and rabbits, running into boar or wolves or bears, falling headlong into a snowdrift, freezing to death.

He breathes deep, waits for his heart to slow, for his imagination to calm down.

Magnus volunteers to join the Urth-bound team, despite the tiny voice in his heart that whispers that he is and always will be a farmer.

Doppelgänger

This is what I am: I'm an explorer of new worlds. I will further the knowledge of our planet. I will be an ambassador, a teacher, an educator. I will be unique.

He dreams of Aerth's twin planet, Urth.

He dreams of Urth-Magnus, his mirror-twin.

He dreams of Urth-Tilly, in love with him.

He dreams of Aerth-Magnus meeting Urth-Magnus.

He dreams the two Magnuses fight, hand to hand, chest to chest, face to face, their hot, slippery bodies more urgent than lovers.

He dreams that one of the Magnuses kills the other, but it's impossible to tell which man dies.

He wakes sweating, his pounding heart his only reassurance.

Holding the heartspace

On the eve of his twenty-sixth birthday Magnus greets Hilden at the main gate of the Space Agency. She's wearing brown woollen trousers and sturdy boots, and a thick waterproof jacket over layers of wool and linen, rather than her usual sage-green robes; she's dressed for warmth, comfort and practicality. She carries a large rucksack on her back, and a small bag in her hand. She has become old, frail, her face deeply lined, her hair thin and white.

'You didn't walk the whole way?'

'Well, I did, naturally.' She smiles at him, and his heart warms. 'I've been meaning to make this pilgrimage for a long time.'

They leave her bags in a guest room and he shows her around: trainees' quarters, family accommodation, lecture rooms, computer hub, rockets, the module he'll be living in for the year's journey to Mars.

There are no secrets here. His mother was wrong to be so suspicious. Nothing is confidential or reserved for those of a certain status. All is open, candid, accessible. Passers-by and schoolchildren have as much right to wander around the base as any scientist or astronaut. We have passed the age of secrets, Hilden reminds Magnus: there are no secrets on Aerth, no need for secrecy, no need to fear enemies, for we have none.

After dinner they stroll in the sandy pine forest outside the city, bathing in the light of the long June evening as a gentle summer frost begins to form. An eagle soars overhead, buzzards circle and curlews call far above in the crystal-blue sky. Hilden has brought two birthday gifts from Magnus's parents, and a hand-painted card of the farmhouse in snow.

The larger gift is a fruit cake, studded with almonds and crystallised orange slices, one of his mother's most special recipes.

'I'll share this with my friends.'

'Certainly,' says Hilden. 'Your parents will expect it.'

'And you'll take letters back for me?'

'I will.'

He'll open the second gift next birthday, on Mars. It's soft and light, wrapped in a hand-dyed neckerchief in rich colours of indigo, scarlet and gold.

Hilden tells Magnus news, most of which he's already heard, but he enjoys discussing it with her, turning it over and examining it from all angles: his mother is living in the Hostel, as happy as she will ever be, her needs met by caring for others and being cared for in turn; his father has joined a farming family at Berkswell, leaving Oak Tree Farm to the mercies of nature; already the forest is recolonising the fields and pastures. It won't be long before bears lift the door latch and enter the kitchen of the unoccupied farmhouse, troops of wild boar eat the abandoned stores of roots and grain, and bees nest in the roof thatch.

'And Tilly?'

Hilden takes his hands in both of hers, this eighty-year-old woman, the keeper of his soul. She squeezes his hands very gently, and says: 'Tilly? Did you not know? Tilly has married, my dear.'

And she wipes his tears as he weeps, and the skylarks sing.

Walk gently

Landing

Landing is tricky. Landing's always tricky.

Magnus has never landed before. He wishes he could practise.

Mars has no oceans. Landing on Mars means careful deployment of balloons and parachutes and reverse thrusters. As they circle the planet, waiting for the landing site to come into view, Magnus wishes he could reverse the thrust of his life.

During the landing he temporarily loses his mind, no, his consciousness; but it might as well be his mind. It might as well.

The way forward is forward

Mars – the gravity? the temperature? the lifestyle? – appears to suit Niall Strong. He seems younger than his sixty-something years, bounding between lab and living quarters, kitchen and horticultural domes. The atmosphere is thin but breathable, with oxygen at 19 per cent, like being at the top of a high mountain on Aerth. Everest, perhaps. The air holds other gases, too: nitrogen, carbon dioxide and argon among others, a historical record of the life once abundant here. People say you can adapt to the low oxygen and low gravity. But today Magnus has his doubts. He feels ancient. Forty years younger than Niall, he staggers around the habitat, nauseous, wobbly with exhaustion.

He ventures outside in his heated suit, feeling as though he may collapse without warning. His oxygen mask dangles around his neck, ready for quick deployment. The temperature is thirty below zero today, and as he tries to take a breath, his throat closes in protest and he chokes, begins to panic.

'Slowly, Magnus,' says Niall, placing his hand on Magnus's shoulder. 'Breathe slower, shallower.' Magnus bends over, sweating with terror, remembering what happens to people when their lungs freeze.

Three breaths. That's enough. Face mask on, nose and mouth covered. *Thank God. Oh, thank God.*

Magnus shudders with the effort of not panicking, not breathing too fast, not screaming in terror, not weeping in regret for where he is, what he has done.

'I should have asked for people of Denisovan ancestry,' says Niall. 'Genetically adapted to breathing thin air. Tibetans, Nepalese. We Anglo-Saxons, we're no good at this. We'll never adapt.'

Magnus stares at him in disbelief.

'Too late now,' continues Niall. 'Have to make do with what we've got.' He straps on a mask and inhales deeply, the skin around his ice-blue eyes crinkling in a smile. 'You'll get your Mars legs,' he says. 'Eventually. Or not.'

These have no meaning at all

Magnus still collects things in his pockets even though he's twenty-six and lives on Mars:

- A rust-coloured rock shaped like a bear, five centimetres long and perfect for holding in his gloved hand as he strides across the red dust;
- Three smooth, almost perfectly spherical pebbles which he's had for ever: a miniature Aerth of royal-blue azurite and fern-green malachite, streaked with white and grey; the second, of blood-red haematite, with wavering lines of black and brown; the last a nondescript biscuit-coloured sandstone, pitted with tiny holes;
- The mysterious and flaking imprint of something (a paw print?) – a promise of life, once, or a dream or hope, which he picked up at the side of what could be, from certain angles, a dried-up riverbed, and which he keeps secret for fear of being laughed at;
- Pliers, dropped by a previous expedition. He should hand these into the stores but likes the heft of them in his pocket;

- ✦ String, from a shed on his family farm: a length of woven twine made of hemp. Why he has brought this with him, he is not at all sure. It has no practical use in such a hostile environment, where steel and aluminium are the materials of practicality amid dust storms and solar radiation;
- ✦ A packet of carrot seed, in case it ever begins to rain.

The astrophysicist's heart

Magnus takes a scalpel and slices open the lacewing pupa. Inside the tough little case he finds a half-formed insect, shrivelled and black. He doesn't bother to examine any of the others. They're beyond hatching, should have hatched weeks ago. Occasionally a moth or other tiny winged creature flutters between the rows of plants in the geodesic domes, but for lack of food or breeding partner they live a day, maybe three days, then fall to the red earth and die.

He longs for the tang of a fresh tomato or the sweetness of a ripe apricot, and spends hours in the greenhouses at night, laboriously transferring pollen from flower to flower with a fine paintbrush. Magnus feels almost paternal about the apple and pear saplings he helped load onto the spacecraft, proud of their achievement in surviving the seven-month voyage, subjected to zero gravity and solar radiation. Eventually a forest of fruit trees will flourish, a planet-wide orchard. That's the plan.

Other crops do better, propagated from roots and cuttings: potatoes, yams, the tubers and leaves of runner beans, the tender flower buds of day lilies, rhubarb, wild garlic, herbs and ginger, perennial kale. Magnus misses eggs and bacon, roast turkey, apple pie, raspberries, chocolate ice cream, smoked salmon, honey. Most of all he misses cake.

He walks between the rows of plants, touching, smelling, tasting. The colours calm him, bringing to mind and heart and body the place he grew up – emerald, forest, jade, the palest beech of tiny banana plants, the darkest pine of potato leaves – and he spends the hour before dinner in the domes, recovering from his day outside, from the dry bitter cold, the wind, the sand, the dust and the rocks, the relentless carmine, scarlet, rust, beige, ochre, tan, butterscotch.

Niall tells the Martian settlers they're going from strength to strength. One day, perhaps in two or three hundred years, they'll be self-sufficient. Weekly, he starts with an anecdote, then a bit of recent tech success, and finally the future, which is upbeat, exciting. Magnus nods in acknowledgement, not agreement, unsure whether these are reasonable projections or wildly over-optimistic.

Magnus gives up his pollination efforts for a day, two days, a week, a month. In his new leisure time, he lies beneath full-grown banana plants as tall as apple trees, gazing up through the glass roof at the rose-gold sky, and dreams of forests, fields and farms.

This feels like betrayal

Magnus finds a tiny extra package tucked inside his birthday present, a letter, folded in on itself in a two-inch square, like a secret. Magnus assumes it's from his mentor Hilden, and is pleased; she writes from the heart, and what she says will be as pertinent now as anything she ever said to him on Aerth, although he does wonder why it had to wait a whole year.

The handmade card has a photograph pasted onto its front of the oak trees behind his parents' farmhouse; the gift is a pair of soft knitted socks, indigo and moss green, a maple leaf embroidered in cornflower blue on the ankle. These are colours Magnus rarely sees these days, textures he never feels. He strokes the wool gently, lays it against his cheek, glad he's alone for a few minutes, that no one witnesses the catch in his breathing and the two or three sniffs which take him by surprise as he sits on his bunk in his regulation uniform, on his regulation bedding.

He peels off his regulation socks and pulls on the woollen ones from home, testing them on the cold concrete floor. Bedsocks, he thinks, as he looks out at a dust devil beginning its whirling dance between rust-red boulders under the copper Martian sky, and feels a momentary nostalgia for home.

But when he opens the note it's not in Hilden's elegant hand; it's a looping scrawl in purple ink, with little hearts and stars and kisses scattered all over. It's a shock, something unbelievable, which Magnus holds by its corners as if it might explode: a letter from Tilly. And it's dated eight years ago, a week before his nineteenth birthday.

She longs to see him, she says, to hold him, kiss him, laugh and talk, walk in the woods together. Winchcombe is *so boring*; she'll come to Thetford and they can live together. *Please, Magnus, say yes, I can't bear to be without you another day.* She misses him so badly, she says; please, please, *please*, write back.

Magnus stares at her words, sweat prickling in his armpits and in his palms, his heart thumping. He can't imagine how this letter came to be included in his parents' gift. Who had it? Who kept it from him? Were there others? This letter – all the letters, for now he's sure there were more – might have altered his life's trajectory.

But it's too late. Eight years and millions of miles too late.

He pulls on his heated outdoor gear. Right now a swift freezing death seems almost attractive. He could switch off the suit and death would come in minutes, but instead he runs uphill through the plantation of tiny conifers. They've grown only a millimetre or two since he arrived on Mars. Success, but hardly measurable, he thinks with sudden scorn, and wonders what he's doing here on this almost lifeless planet, when all this time he could have been at home with Tilly. What with truth, and love, and *no harm*, he can't understand how this letter has arrived in his hands.

Magnus runs as far as his oxygen allows, and pulls off his mask. He howls in rage and grief at both moons rising, then drops breathless to his hands and knees. Before him is a miniature Scots pine, bent sideways by the constant wind and coated in red dust like bloody snow. He scrabbles with his thick grey gloves at the base of the foot-high tree, and buries Tilly's letter in the dirt.

Missing

There have been other girls since Tilly, but none of them fit that Tilly-shaped place in Magnus's heart.

Everything's just marvellous

After building a vast radio array, Mars is able to receive better-quality information from Urth, in larger quantities: music, art and films; nature documentaries, cultural commentaries, the biographies of many great men and a few great women. Magnus gets stuck in, spends hours watching, listening, absorbing. The planet is astonishingly beautiful, and astonishingly like Aerth.

The planets are similar beyond all possibility of coincidence – land masses and oceans, flora and fauna, languages and cultures. The main difference is its geopolitics, a term no longer used on Aerth and which nobody really understands. And the very different population numbers. And the climates. There are indications that Urth is warming rapidly, unlike

Aerth, which is cooling rapidly. Magnus dismisses this as of no concern. In fact the opposite is true; it's exciting. Clearly Urth has escaped the hell that is an ice age.

In the evenings he stares into the night sky, seeking the pale grey dot that is Urth. Somehow this feels more authentic than using a telescope, reminds him of gazing up at the Milky Way when he was a child. Urth tugs at him, as if it's waiting for him, as if this is what he's been looking for all his life, as if he's going home.

He aches to go barefoot on lush grass or hot sand, the sun warming his naked body. He pictures birds and wild creatures – meercats, mice, marmosets – eating nuts and berries from his hands. He dreams of picnics by crystal clear streams, the sweet juice of Urthian fruits: pomegranates, grapes, mangoes and oranges he'll harvest himself from trees growing in the fertile soils of this warm and welcoming planet. He regrets nothing, regrets not one day of the last eight tough years.

His stomach flutters and churns at the thought of first contact. He loses his appetite, loses weight and is in danger of being dropped from the mission: months of travel, a whole year on Urth, months coming back. He reminds himself sternly there's nothing left for him on Aerth, and forces himself to eat, to get fit, ignoring the fact that he's ignoring his tiny internal whisper of love and truth.

The day before he leaves, Magnus takes off the weights at his ankles, wrists, waist and in the low Martian gravity bounds up the hill to a miniature wind-distorted Scots pine. He scrabbles in the red dust at its base for Tilly's letter. Opening his four layers of heated clothing to the minus-thirty-degree air, he tucks the precious colder-than-ice square of paper under his vest, next to his skin. The dirt stains his gloves the colour of dried blood.

Live truth

Splashdown

Splashing down. It sounds soft, like a baby's bath.

Magnus imagines the gentleness of bathwater, raindrops, streams and brooks… water that trickles and flows, that buoys and tugs, that pulls and pushes, cools and refreshes.

He contains his breathing, controls it: in, out, in, out; counts the breaths, the seconds; watches the instruments, watches his four fellow astronauts crammed into the tiny capsule, watches the planet beneath them.

Blue flames flicker around the edges of his little window as the capsule falls through the upper atmosphere at four hundred miles an hour.

Mountains, deserts, cloud. Cities, grey, uneven, jagged things along the seashores, like lichen or mould. He looks in vain for green or blue among the shades of brown and grey.

They've been taught about friction fire, the heat and the discomfort, but it's another thing entirely to see it, to feel it. To hear the groaning of the metal. To feel faint with vertigo, to fear you're being cooked alive.

Thank all the engineers on both planets the capsule's landing in water.

Fast and faster…

Falling, tumbling, turning…
He shouts: *Parachutes?*

No one shouts back. Did he even utter a word?

Can't worry now, too late, too late.

Flames streak scarlet and yellow against the window.

Hot and hotter…

Stench of burning
searing

scorching

Sweat trickles down his back, between his buttocks, under his arms, drenches his face and neck.

With difficulty Magnus turns his head.

Florian's eyes are closed, his face white. Hair wet. Sweat streaming.

Capsule's turning, plummeting. Straps digging in.

Ocean rushing up impossibly big

We're landing where there?

There?

Black water surges up, infinite bottomless like black space trapping light no life no no no

Can't turn head ***can't*** breathe ***can't*** hear ***can't*** see

Where friends where there no where nowhere?

Alive… dead…?

conscious unconscious

breathing suffocating

Ears roar

Eyes spot black red

Blood roars spots stains

bleeds

HELP

Nausea sick

vomitous

stabbing in head

gravity pressure

juddering

shaking

throwing about

throwing up

capsule disintegrating would be kindness

really it would

really please oh please

Oh God if there's a God please oh God

BlackwaterHugeSolidLIKEHITTING
CONCRETE

Teamwork

From your single room in the hospital you ask to see your team but are told that's not possible. Various reasons are given: rest, sleep, surgery. Induced coma.

People peer at you through the little window in your door, just as you peered through your little window in the space capsule. You can read nothing in their eyes. The people are uncannily Aerth-like, even calling themselves human. Their language is odd only in the accent. You can communicate with the nursing staff, clad head to toe in white baggy suits with hoods and visors and gloves. Whether you understand each other is a different matter.

Your room is a white cube. It has no view onto the outside world; the walls are stark and plain, the angles hard and accurate. Machines hum and beep, and a camera blinks its tiny red eye at you once a second. 86,400 times a day. The bright overhead light dims at a bedtime chosen by others. Perhaps you're underground. You'd love to see the stars.

You pick at food, fancying none of it except pineapple, which you've never eaten before and which hits the spot. You try to sleep, but nausea – and pain – and noise in the corridor – and anxiety – keep you wakeful.

Occasionally you visit other parts of the hospital, and that's a challenge, getting into a wheelchair with your broken feet. Held around your chest and legs you are lifted, dangled and dropped, and strapped in. A nurse trundles you down bright white-and-grey corridors, lit by fluorescent tubes fastened to the ceilings. You reach shining metal doors which slide open at a button's touch onto small, boxlike spaces. The box ascends, or descends, and you're always hopeful that this time you may reach a place where you can see daylight, the outside of this building, a tiny fraction of the planet you glimpsed from miles above the surface. You ask again about your team – *How are they getting on?* – but the reply is vague and general, and you swallow your disappointment, resolve to remember every detail so that when you finally meet you can compare notes, compile a summary of this alien beginning.

And blood is taken, many times; and your blood pressure and temperature monitored; and people measure the strength of your muscles – hardly fair, you've been in low gravity for months – and push you inside long, noisy tubes which pulsate claustrophobically. Sometimes they tell you what's happening, but you can never remember afterwards.

You ask about fresh air, feeling the sun on your face and the wind in your hair. You wouldn't mind if it was wet or snowing, you add. People remain vague. Soon, they say, soon, and their eyes slide away. Perhaps you have been too lyrical, too romantic for these technocrats; perhaps they don't understand your need for connection with the natural world. Nor your intense curiosity.

One day you feel a surge of energy – at last! – so you let down the metal rail on the side of your bed and swing out your legs. But your ankles are unable to bear your weight and you fall, pain searing up your legs and your spine and into your head. You cry out, your face crushed against the shiny grey floor. The door opens, two people rush in and kneel beside you, call for a third who takes your legs, and they lift you gently onto the firm bed, raise the safety rail, say to each other: 'Fell out', 'Safety rail down', 'Who last checked on him?' And to you, 'You're all right, we've got you, it's OK', as if speaking to a child or a pet.

They tell you not to worry, you're never alone, you need to rest, regain your strength; there are three dedicated teams, on rotation, day and night. You're OK.

Not really OK. You have learned that expression by hearing it from the Urthians. Not OK at all.

Insomnia

Magnus can't sleep. He shuffles along the hospital corridors on his bandaged feet, hoping the pain from the steel pins in his ankles will exhaust him.

Florian and Justina lie side by side on metal tables, covered in white sheets. They look as if they are asleep.

Nerina lies so deeply asleep it is doubtful that she will ever wake. Her blonde curls are spread out on a white pillow; her pink mouth is firmly closed. Magnus regrets he didn't get to know that mouth better. He leans forward and brushes her lips with his own.

Athelstan has lost the ability to speak or move, and spends hours crying like a baby. He calms only when Magnus clambers onto the bed alongside him, takes him in his arms and gently rocks him. They both, finally, sleep.

Matriarchy

Magnus is well enough for a quick debrief, but not well enough to go outside. His name, he tells the ten men and one woman on the opposite side of the long shiny black table, is Magnus of Arden. He watches the woman take notes. She smiles at him when she looks up, so he addresses his answers to her.

'Magnus Ovarden?' repeats an older man with silver-framed glasses.

'Magnus of Arden,' says Magnus. 'That's my name. Magnus. Of. Arden.'

'Of Arden?'

Magnus nods.

'That's your surname? Arden?'

'Surname?'

'Your family name?'

'Yes. My whole family. Apart from other family members who don't live near us.'

The man nods. The woman makes a note.

Magnus takes a chocolate biscuit and reaches towards the mug of coffee in front of him.

'No,' says the man. 'Don't drink that. It's cold.' He turns to the woman, who rises and leaves the room.

'I come from Arden,' adds Magnus, hoping to clarify matters. He can't imagine why the person in charge has left. He hardly dares to hope she might offer to take him to a place like Arden. He could badly do with walking in a forest. Sooner rather than later. But it might not happen if she doesn't hear it. 'Meriden. It's forested. Bears, wolves. You see elk, sometimes. And lynx. There are beavers.'

The people look polite.

'Does Meriden exist here? Could I visit?'

The people glance at each other. The man says, 'Certainly. I believe it's a large suburb of Birmingham. You won't find any woods, I'm afraid.'

Woods aren't the same as forests, but before Magnus can say so, the man speaks again.

'Magnus Arden.'

'Magnus of Arden,' says Magnus.

The people nod.

The woman comes back with fresh coffee and more biscuits. She comes round to his place and pours him a mug.

The press release names him as Commander Magnus Ovarden.

Of the five astronauts, only Magnus remains. This news is broken to him by a doctor wearing civilian clothing and without face mask or visor, whose office has a window onto lofty buildings crowding close like trees in a pine forest, blocking any light.

Magnus can't think what to say. Shock and relief grapple within him, relief that his friends' suffering is over, shock that he'll be navigating this planet alone. He feels guilt, too, that his leadership didn't protect them.

The doctor's name is Edward. He is very sorry. He knows this must be difficult. He can be available at any time, if Magnus needs to talk. Is there anything right now that Magnus would like to discuss or explore? Any questions that he, Edward, can answer? Edward is skilled at helping people process their emotions. He is a psychiatrist. Perhaps this role exists on Aerth, too?

Magnus is numb. Edward is expectant, concerned, his eyebrows slightly furrowed. He leans forward in his chair, hands clasped.

Magnus feels he should put Edward at ease. He asks about Edward's lack of mask.

Edward looks surprised, leans back, says that tests have shown that Magnus is not infectious. Edward has been in isolation to ensure that he, too, carries no infectious disease. And in any case, Magnus needs to build up his immunity to Urthly infections.

A year, thinks Magnus, a whole year here, alone; and he doesn't know if he feels good or bad about that. He thanks Edward for his time.

He slides his bandaged feet along the glossy corridor to a room with a narrow horizontal window, placed high. A nurse pushes a wheelchair behind him. There are armchairs and low tables, jigsaw puzzles and a few battered books.

Magnus lets go of the door, takes three actual paces into a patch of sun, welcoming and warm like an embrace. If his feet weren't so broken, if he weren't grieving, he'd do a little dance of delight at this promise from outside.

He lifts his face to the sunlight, remembers Aerth millions of miles beyond, remembers his training, remembers his parents and their – yes, he sees it now – their sacrifice. Sombre, he closes his eyes, makes a resolution. He'll do more than grieve; he'll honour his team by exploring, learning, tasting everything this new world has to offer.

Magnus settles in an armchair. The nurse asks about coffee or tea, but he tried a hot drink from the machine in the corridor last week and found it disgusting. This planet doesn't understand food.

On the silent TV, men walk in a forest. There are children and women in vegetable gardens, hoeing and weeding and harvesting. They feed chickens, gather eggs, milk cows by hand, such familiar actions that Magnus settles to watch, obscurely comforted.

Some men talk together, seriously. Others join them. They seem to hear noises, stop talking, look around.

Women and children run into the houses, hide under beds and inside wardrobes. The men gather farm tools and rifles, shout silently, faces contorted in anger or distress.

Magnus feels his pulse thud faster, his breathing become rapid and shallow. He attempts to lever himself out of the chair to turn up the sound. The nurse gets there before him, moves close to the TV so he can't see the screen. He leans sideways to peer around her.

Magnus catches his breath, says, What?

It's just a movie, she says.

On the screen behind her, men in black uniforms and helmets bash people over the head with thick wide sticks, like bashing fenceposts into the ground.

They're kicking people, like kicking cabbages around a field.

They're hauling people over the soil, like hauling logs out of the forest.

But what? Magnus asks again. I don't know what they're doing. Why are they doing this?

The nurse turns off the TV. It's time for dinner.

Curfew

A dank, muggy night, warm enough to sweat. Weak pools of light from street lamps. The massive bulk of monolithic buildings. A strong smell, something acrid. A kind of burning smell. Sewage.

Shaky with nerves, for the first time in his life Magnus steps into a large black automobile, where he registers with surprise another passenger. He reminds himself not to stare. He saw this type of face in old picture books when he was a child. From his name badge he is Doctor Wu. There's also a man with dark skin, a physiotherapist he's met before. And, reassuringly, a woman. She must be the team leader.

Two burly men enter the vehicle. They lock the doors and tell the driver to drive.

It's after midnight and there's a *curfew*. A word unknown to Magnus, so he asks what it is, and Doctor Wu laughs and says, *This!*

No wiser, Magnus turns to the window, to empty streets and darkened buildings. The automobile accelerates.

Oh.

My.

Heart.

The excitement. The fear. The adrenaline.

Huge buildings speed by, lights disappear in a blur. Sometimes the automobile slows and he glimpses people in doorways. He turns to Doctor Wu and says *Curfew?* Doctor Wu shakes his head. Magnus leans forward, asks the woman. One of the burly men sitting in front speaks over the noise of the engine. He doesn't bother to turn around. *To control bad people. Criminals. Immigrants.*

Bad people. Magnus ponders this while the automobile speeds up. Eighty kilometres an hour, eighty-five. Ninety. He peers behind him at the road. No vehicles. Maybe the bad people are ashamed of being seen. Maybe they use this time to learn how not to be bad. He can't imagine what badness looks like, unless it's like the people in the movie. And it's late, anyway. Everyone must be in bed.

Now they join a highway, wide like a great river, blank and empty. One hundred and thirty kilometres an hour.

Buckle up, one of the bulky men says to Magnus.

Magnus has no idea what he means. Doctor Wu pulls a strap from behind Magnus's shoulder and snaps it shut across his lap. Safety. Basic.

They turn off the highway, begin a fast, lurching ride along a curving road. Then metal gates, torchlight flashing on his face, men's voices, dogs barking.

Dogs! Great, tomorrow he can play with dogs!

They drive more slowly, and stop. Helped out of the vehicle, Magnus stands tall despite his aching ankles, notices first the people lined up waiting to greet him, then the mansion beyond. A flight of steps, big open doors. Massive windows. Spotlights illuminating the facade, the statues, the stone ornamentation, the columns. He has seen places like this in documentaries. What a beauty.

For your convalescence, says Doctor Wu.

Magnus breathes deep. The air smells not quite fresh. But there is the tiniest scent of trees on the breeze – pine and yes, oak and beech – and dry grass, and something floral. Roses, maybe. *Just give me a few days*, he says.

Doctor Wu merely smiles, and Magnus can read nothing in his eyes, in the half-dark, in the shadows.

The great, the good

In an immense room filled with dozens of people, long platters of food are laid on white-clothed tables, men and women carry drinks on trays. There are grapes! Aubergines! Tiny bell peppers filled with cream cheese… small cubes of fish and herbs… little rolls of bacon and peaches… miniature loaves of bread stuffed with so many fillings that Magnus loses count… cakes and pastries. The hospital food was clearly an aberration. Urthians do know how to cook.

The crowd falls silent, listening to a man who welcomes Magnus to Urth, to his first official engagement. Magnus thanks him, smiles at the crowd. He doesn't eat – it would be rude when everyone is looking at him, when a speech is being made, when a feast has been prepared. There are more speeches, from more men, some in uniform, some in robes. There is a great deal of clapping.

When the first man speaks again, telling the crowd to enjoy their lunch, people cluster around Magnus, queue to meet him. They shake his hand, tell him how much they've been looking forward to this occasion, and is he feeling better? He nods and smiles while his empty stomach rumbles. Someone gives him a fizzing drink that pricks his nose and throat, surprising him with its perfumed astringency. A man refills his glass constantly, from a bottle covered in beads of condensation. He can't interrupt the people's kind questioning to squeeze through the crowd in pursuit of lunch, so he drinks his fizzy drink and tries to keep up with what people are saying, in their strange accents, talking over each other, desperate to catch his eye.

At some unknown signal the food is cleared away, hardly touched. The guests disperse to vehicles on the gravel outside. Magnus turns to gather some of the little snacks before they disappear, but he feels light-headed, dizzy, and he stumbles. Doctor Wu leads him to a wheelchair.

Upstairs, Doctor Wu tells Magnus to sleep, arranges for tea to be brought to his vast bedroom at four o'clock.

'What happened to the food downstairs?' Magnus asks.

Doctor Wu looks mildly surprised. 'I suspect it will be thrown away.'

Magnus presses a cushion against his rumbling stomach, glad he ate breakfast, and wonders at the wealth of a planet where food is discarded without a backward glance.

(Dis)Connection

Magnus wheels himself to the plate glass window and peers down at London, seventy storeys below. The vast city seems tiny, inconsequential, irrelevant to his emotions and bodily sensations. Right now his stomach is rumbling, for example. Right now he feels lost, abandoned. Right now he feels as if he might slip through the atoms of the reinforced glass and float down to the waiting crowds.

He presses his face to the glass, squinting to see the streets.

Minute vehicles crawl along like beetles, humans even slower, like dust mites. At ground level the city overpowers him: eager faces press close; strident voices call his name, hungry for his reactions; the acrid smell of dirt and diesel, the grime, the litter, the grey. The cameras.

'Enjoying yourself?'

He turns his wheelchair to face a woman. She crouches beside him. 'Are you?' he asks.

She raises her eyebrows almost imperceptibly and gives him a tiny smile. Behind her the room tilts further. He closes his eyes.

'Not feeling so good,' he hears her say to someone, not him. She swings his chair around and he's gliding across the smooth marble floor. He opens his eyes as they go through the giant double doors towards the glass lift, and, gazing at the woman rather than the view, he feels himself plummet.

Synaesthesia

So many impressions, so much to absorb.

Copters – the deafening scarlet of spinning blades, the sunflower-yellow vertiginous lifting and dropping onto fields, gardens and rooftops. The pervasive sludge-coloured smell of sweat and fear.

A pebbly beach, a clifftop, a wild storm, a slate-coloured sea. Salt on his tongue and lips, vanilla.

Women, wealthy women: dazzling lilac-scented butterflies

in bright silks and linens, eyes and lips exotically coloured, adorned with glowing jewels; women with staff, servants, time and leisure; soft silkiness, the taste and texture of macarons.

Men. Powerful men, Magnus belatedly realises. Charming, erudite, attentive, flattering, seeking information. They move slowly, deliberately, in dark, serious clothing. The feel of a smooth steel blade.

Woodland, forests, the trees sparse-clad, dry and brittle, the dust making him sneeze, the fallen bark crumbling beneath his feet.

Population, a pulsating flashing alarm, the sour tang of poverty, drab and dull. Magnus gasps at the daily birth rates, the average age at death. He is advised not to concern himself. These things are not within Magnus's purview. Experts will prepare a report for Aerth, and Magnus will occupy himself with culture.

Galleries, concerts. A kaleidoscope of colours. Instruments he has never heard before – the saxophone, the electric guitar, the organ, the sitar. Good wine, expensive canapés. He glimpses sprawling towns and cities in monochrome, places not within his *purview*.

Hot, cold, wet, thirsty, hungry, headachy, nauseous, exhausted, confused.

Water. Rain, relentless. Rivers rising in sheets, submerging towns, villages, fields. All the many colours and tastes of mud.

The juice of the grape, its potency unexpected, its legacy treated with analgesics, electrolytes, water and sausages: a blinding white searchlight; nausea, orange juice, pork fat.

Stunning houses, marble interiors, the palest cream and grey. Carefully tended gardens, verdant against a backdrop of dust and scorch. The sharp smell of new-mown grass. His every whim indulged – raspberry sorbet at 2 a.m. – within a relentless timetable of appointments over which he has no control.

Computational devices. Hard, cool, bright. Easy to use, addictive. Stiff neck, dry eyes, insomnia, headaches.

The weather. Oh, the weather. Never quite knowing what it will be. Tornadoes yielding to spring buds unfurling in gentle sunshine; sweaty, humid air; randomly destructive hailstones in multiple sizes; soft drizzle; hair-frizzling static; electrical storms; terrifying cloudbursts and violent floods; a sun that sets the world literally ablaze.

His growing loneliness, a quiet sepia. The hot stinging crimson of the inside of his eyelids.

Mentor

Greater Britain's boundaries reach Alaska in one direction and Prussia in the other, together with all the West and East Indies, Persia, and certain minor territories across the globe – although of course these often change, adds the adviser walking with Magnus towards the Prime Minister's office. They've met once before, at the reception, but Magnus remembers little of that day.

In his office the PM quizzes him about life on Aerth.

'I need to impress upon you, Magnus, that we must learn from you at least as much as you learn from us. We will make good use of any information you share, better use than any of our overseas colleagues. You can trust me on that.'

Magnus does trust the Prime Minister, despite his inherent caution about male leadership. Trust is built into the very core of him, like the heartwood of an ancient tree. He's mildly surprised that trust needs to be mentioned.

The PM taps a file on his desk.

'Your planet's space programme is quite frankly astonishing. So primitive! Rockets held together by string and chewing gum. Hah! And no internet… hard to believe. Such old technology… radio… dial-up phones… cathode ray tubes… transistors… I have absolutely no idea how you managed to get here, let alone build things on Mars – which, by the way, we need to discuss. No wonder your colleagues died. Wings and prayers come to mind. Hah!'

The Prime Minister doesn't strike Magnus as a man who prays.

'I hear you're good on farming in sub-Arctic conditions! But seriously, some religious leaders are interested in your social systems. We won't adopt them here. We're too advanced.'

Magnus feels buffeted. He mentions that he could do with a mentor.

'Indeed. Meanwhile, we'd like you to travel, do a global tour. Meet people, experience our world. How do you feel about that, Magnus?'

Magnus's heart leaps. He's astonished, delighted, thrilled. All his boyhood dreams are about to be realised. What experiences he'll have, what stories he'll tell! He grins. 'It would be an honour,' he says. Adds, 'Sir.'

'Splendid! We'll get you on a plane tomorrow. Won't see you for a few weeks, but you'll be well looked after.' The Prime Minister turns away, picks up a document, his glasses perched on his nose.

Magnus smiles, looks around the room to see who he's travelling with, which female elder will be advising him, but faces remain blank, expressionless.

Wild, at heart

Magnus circles Urth like an albatross, barely touching down. Watching the planet roll beneath the clouds he closes his eyes and braces himself for landing, his throat tightening, his stomach churning, but each time it's smooth and uneventful, the plane gliding along the runway so gently he's often unaware they've arrived.

Driven through screaming crowds by limousine – or jeep or taxi, or once, memorably, by military tank – Magnus finds himself walking red carpets at charity fundraisers and movie premieres; appearing on news programmes and chat shows; visiting the great monuments, ancient sites and famous treasures of the world; whistling in and out of schools, hospitals and colleges; riding in cavalcades with politicians. Everywhere, he is protected by outriders and snipers and men with dark glasses and handguns.

He lands, he shakes hands, he flies off again, whisked from one grey monochrome environment to another, hard matte surfaces offset by glittering glass, steel and plastic, the bitter air cloudy with acrid dust and particles which make him cough.

Magnus asks for a face mask, like those worn by people whose gloved hands reach out to him across crowd barriers.

An official refuses the mask, says it wouldn't be good PR. People need to see his face, need to know he's real, that he's not a publicity stunt for a movie studio or government.

Magnus develops a cough and that's not good PR at all.

He asks for colour, for scent, for the indigenous, for fresh air: art, temples, lakes and mountains, forests and markets and dancing and delicious foods, things he's seen in documentaries. Something a little more authentic, meaningful, original, something to help his soul sing, that may help him sleep at night.

An arrangement is made for Magnus to holiday a little.

He encounters villages of dancing maidens and spear-wielding men; eats spicy food in empty restaurants scrutinised by local people at a respectful distance; rides in a canoe up a swirling muddy ocean-wide river behind a half-naked brown man who paddles against the current, his phone tucked into grubby blue nylon shorts.

Dolphins used to swim in this river, but when Magnus asks, nobody knows what happened to them.

And there's the rainforest:
A hundred tall trees
stand alone,
vulnerable,
beyond the scrub,
beyond the airport,

beyond reach.

Lucky

When Magnus blows his nose the tissue is filled with black slime, and he needs to take a shower twice a day. The few patches of grass and the occasional tree simply look depressed. Rats scuttle between bins. Grimy people sprawl on benches surrounded by bulging bags, and drivers and security guards are reticent about them, like they're reticent about war, poverty, deforestation, fossil fuels.

It's not that they don't know about these things, it's more that – Magnus senses – they don't know what to say, exactly, that might not (a) confuse him or (b) get themselves into trouble.

But it's a great job, says one: regular work, travelling, meeting people, having experiences he could only dream of before it all goes tits up. He wouldn't want to lose this job.

What is 'tits up', Magnus asks, but the man says, It's nothing, nothing, forget it. It's just a joke. Don't tell anyone. What do you want to do with all this crap? Sell it? He gestures at the boxes stacked like walls around the apartment, gifts from admirers. Magnus has kept the houseplants, placed the fruit in his fridge, eaten some of the food.

You can have it, says Magnus. I don't need it.

Things are going really well

Communication with Aerth is possible only when Mars is aligned with both Aerth and Urth, and is always affected by solar radiation, dust storms, the clumping of ionospheric particles on any of the three planets, Urth's regular hurricanes, electrical cloud cover and swarms of locusts. Magnus isn't sure about this last point, but someone – he can't remember who – assured him it was true, and laughed.

He writes home, wishing he could speak to his parents face to face, wishing he could hug them. Although their relationship shifted tectonically in the years before he joined the Space Agency, it improved before he left Aerth, once he recognised that all they ever wanted was the very best for him. He longs for them now, like a small child. It will be weeks before he hears back, if at all. He crafts each message carefully, indicating that it's all been worthwhile: the long years of training, the danger, the separation from loved ones. It's a kind of destiny, he conveys, and Magnus has always been exactly the right kind of Aerthian adventurer.

Magnus doesn't dwell on how desperately he misses his mother and father, his village, his friends. The quiet routine of their lives. Or that he doesn't quite believe his own words. Besides, getting through each day takes all his energy, on this chaotic, teeming, crowded world.

- Art galleries, classical concerts, gardens: astonishing, he could stay there all day!!!
- Stately homes: empty buildings that could house a thousand!!!
- London: huge, important, not a collection of marshy villages!!!
- TV: hundreds of channels, not one!!!
- The news!!! 24 hours a day!!!

He avoids or circumnavigates other topics:

Rock concerts… reality shows on TV… clubs and bars… the competitive consumption of alcohol, like a sport. And women: their mystery, the fashions, the hairstyles, the make-up.

Then there's the transport, in multiple forms, hurried, harried, stressful, fast, slow, rarely on time… And medicine – industrial, costly, hard to get… And the news! Constant, depressing, confusing, and quite honestly grim, unless it's about celebrities. And they, along with politicians and people famous for just about anything, are two a penny.

He has looked in vain for decent forests, meadows and orchards, has found few wild animals, birds or insects. He hugs this knowledge to himself, buries it deep like a bad dream, looks forward to returning home.

The darker moments

Magnus lives alone in an official apartment on a prime London site alongside a regrettably polluted River Thames, where he lies awake, listing his lonelinesses:

✦ Being the only survivor.

✦ TV stations expecting him to be an expert on world affairs, culture, science, and, of all things, religion.

✦ Fan mail. Poetry. Love letters. Proposals of marriage. Photos of people's pets/children. Holiday postcards. Sent to the PM's office and brought round by the staff.

✦ Vanloads transported by world-weary security guards: taxidermied animals; unwashed underwear; boxes of foodstuffs; wine; beer; lager; cider; spirits; business propositions accompanied by working prototypes; baskets of fresh fruit; collectable figurines; clothing and shoes; houseplants.

✦ Small crowds demonstrating with placards:

Spaceman Go Home.

✦ The Flat Urth Society turning up to point out that clearly he comes from the land of ice beyond Antarctica.

✦ So many books being written about him, within months his face on dust jackets in bookshop windows.

✦ So many songs sung.

✦ So many comedy shows. The butt of a thousand jokes. Being told he hasn't got a sense of humour if he doesn't laugh.

✦ Rumours about his plans to destroy the planet.

✦ Schools begging him to open their sports days or summer fetes.

✦ Begging letters citing worthy charities/personal needs/mad schemes to improve the world. He's thankful he has no money.

✦ Going everywhere with security guards. People bothering him all the time. His face on the sides of buses.

✦ Aerth movies in which the men are unnaturally hairy and the women unusually beautiful, and they dress in leather and sheepskin and live in houses which look strangely like caves.

✦ Missing everyone at home. Wishing – sometimes – he hadn't come. Resolving, always, to do better.

This isn't how you thought it would be

The mighty Thames, navigated by great empires, is solid with rubbish. Dead animals – foxes and cats, magpies and pigeons – drift among the plastic bottles and refuse bags. Revolted, Magnus turns to another bedroom, but this gives him the uncomfortable sense of being observed from windows across the road.

A quiet female AI voice, programmed with his own accent, greets him by name when he enters a room and says goodbye when he leaves; it makes him irritable and homesick until he succeeds in turning it off (not easy to find, that command), but it resumes automatically after midnight and whenever he returns to the apartment. When he sits quietly with a book or a movie, and the AI woman is quiet too, he succeeds in putting his homesickness out of his mind for minutes at a time.

It's raining today, raindrops fused together like rods of grey steel, pounding relentlessly on his roof terrace. His tiny olive tree, his roses, herbs, cabbages and lettuces, plants he chose with such love and care at the garden centre, lie broken and crushed across the edges of the wooden tubs and troughs.

He makes coffee and watches the news. Although thrilled when he first found channels dedicated to current affairs, now they depress him; nothing like these exist on Aerth, and if they did, they would surely be different. There'd be positive stories, stories that didn't make him want to throw himself into the filthy river or jump out of the window watched by his unseen watchers.

The alternately sober and cheery newsreaders speak of fifteen hurricanes and tropical storms around the planet's waist like a chain-link belt; elections tainted by vote-rigging accusations; military service extended by five years; an international fashion house facing bankruptcy; the drought continuing in the Middle East, deserts encroaching. Elsewhere – they always say that, *Elsewhere* – heavy rains bring landslides, villages are swept away by soil and rubble, people drown in liquid mud which hardens like concrete around them. Magnus tries to imagine this horror, to have empathy, but his mind squirms away, refusing to focus.

Now the newsreaders move to lighter topics. Sporting successes, a rock star's new marriage. A social media sensation: dogs bouncing on trampolines. Adverts: foods, holidays, perfumes, airlines, disaster movies.

Magnus stares at the TV, coffee in hand. His headache throbs in time with his pulse. He should eat, but he is queasy at the thought.

Breaking news runs across the screen: HURRICANE UPGRADED TO CATEGORY 7.

Magnus needs to get out, to leave this stifling, claustrophobic overwhelm, to find a place to walk, trees, grass. He takes his coffee to the door, and touches the handle.

The AI woman says: 'Don't forget your waterproof coat and shoes, Magnus. Remember your umbrella.'

'I turned you off.'

'This is an emergency. Your commands are overridden in an emergency, Magnus.'

Magnus places his hand on the door. Made from genuine engineered oak, it is reinforced with hidden steel bars and bolts on each side, but the oak is unnaturally smooth, the grain visible but disconcertingly imperceptible to his fingertips through its plastic coating. He considers the level of security in the apartment. 'Not an emergency,' he says.

He ignores the AI, which is repeating its recommendations about waterproofs and umbrella, opens the door and takes his coffee down to the flooded street. He sloshes through the drenching rain to a bench in the park, where he stays till dark, sodden and cold, watched by two men sitting opposite under the dripping trees, and he strains to hear the words whispering in his heart

The expert speaks

Journalists wonder openly how technologically primitive Aerth managed to send a small space capsule millions of miles across the solar system. They ask Magnus what insights in tech, or computing, or medicine, or economics, or industry – or any number of things – he can bring to the table.

Magnus is so in awe of Urth's developments (minuscule computational devices disguised as spectacles, bionic body parts, DNA engineering for health and cosmetics, geoengineering to prevent natural disasters, atmosphere-scrubbing particles that are utterly inert, so the inventors say) that all thoughts of Aerthian insights disappear from his mind. He occasionally mentions the rules for life he grew up with, and people stare through him as if he is a piece of glass. He explains that Aerth did away with all monetary systems many decades ago, is then quizzed about healthcare, housing and entertainment, and confirms that yes, it's all free. Then how are things paid for? He says that's a meaningless question, and smiles at baffled faces who don't smile back.

Behind all the scenes, Urth has stepped up communication with Aerth, learning where the two planets' histories diverge, how it is that language is so similar yet development so different; how slight variances in geography have given rise to contrasting trajectories of empires and states; why philosophy of selfhood is so individualistic on one planet and so self-abnegating on the other. Across millions of miles the radio signals sometimes reach their destination, sometimes not. Patience is required, and confusion is almost guaranteed.

'I'm an ordinary man, with an extraordinary story,' says Magnus. 'A huge piece of good fortune propelled me here. I was chosen because I was willing and able.'

'Convenient that your colleagues died,' says one of a group.

Magnus stares. 'I wish they hadn't,' he says, but the group is already walking away.

The grapevine of behind-the-scenes informs the world that Aerthian history is not straightforward, that there may be secrets Aerth would not like revealed. Private discussions are taking place at the highest level. Magnus, confident in his planet's values, states that there is nothing to be suspicious about.

'Yes, there were other civilisations on Aerth many centuries ago. Civilisations have a natural life cycle: a few hundred years of growth, a few hundred years consolidating, a few hundred years of decline…

'Sometimes decline happens quickly, that's correct. Oh no, not just a decade, not at all. And don't forget that Aerth is approaching a glacial maximum…

'Collapse? I wouldn't call it that – I'm sorry?…

'I assure you there's nothing sinister about Aerth's virus. It came in two great waves in the last century. There were earlier, localised waves, you're right…

'Oh, centuries ago. Tragic, yes, absolutely…

'Probably zoonotic…

'What, me personally? I was taught about it in school. It's a major topic in the curriculum…

'I'm very well informed…

'I'm very fortunate, very healthy…

'Not make the same mistake again? I'm sorry, what mistake are you referring to?'

Nobody knows anything

Urth is twin to Aerth in almost every respect, except the climate. Even the geography is roughly as you'd expect, despite the lack of rainforest (Urth) and the approaching ice age

(Aerth). No explanations make sense to Magnus, even after consulting with geologists and astrophysicists, who are mostly bothered that his accounts of Mars don't tally with what they know. Magnus assures them that Mars has a magnetic field and an atmosphere; below ground there is flowing water in which fish-like creatures swim, and primitive life on the surface – single-celled organisms and lichen-like plants. They stumble at this inconsistency, which they can't corroborate with their instruments. The Mars they see has no life, is barren and dead.

Magnus finds oddly designed websites sporting theories concerning Möbius strips and wormholes, or unsubstantiated claims that he is part of an international conspiracy, a kind of bread-and-circuses distraction from famine, global bankruptcy and climate catastrophe, to put it baldly, although nobody ever does.

But Magnus has more pressing concerns, fears that keep him up at night surfing the blogs of crazy guys who seem to post at exactly the moment he tunes in.

Could this planetary twinness mean that another version of him, an Urthian Magnus, walks this planet? What if they were to meet, bump into each other on a crowded street? Would they pass each other by, looking askance? Or greet each other like long-lost brothers?

Or… might they cancel each other out? Might the universe explode into countless atoms? Might it be as if neither world had ever existed? In which case nobody would know anything about it. In which case there's nothing to worry about.

Life on Urth

Journalists discover it's Magnus's birthday, take him to dinner at a club. There's far too much alcohol and his head swims. A pretty girl offers him drugs. He likes the look of her, but not the look of madness descending on the people at his table. He tries to leave several times, is photographed with individuals he doesn't know who drape their arms around his shoulders, give him exaggerated kisses on his cheeks, their eyes on the cameras. He knows he'll feature in tomorrow's news, looking serious and tired. He's a celebrity, after all.

He has never felt more lonely.

Before he collapses into bed Magnus decides not to watch his parents' video. He knows how it will play.

They will sing 'Happy Birthday'. They'll cut an iced cake after blowing out thirty slender birthday candles, one for each of the years of his life. His mother will cry.

At this point Magnus will skip to the end, unable to bear his mother's tears and his father's helplessness.

In a postscript, recorded by his father alone, his father will tell Magnus how proud he is. *You're a pioneer*, his father will say. *If only I'd been younger…*

The same happened each year during his training. It's as if they recorded the videos en masse.

This may have been the plan all along

The canaries cheep and flutter from perch to perch as the Prime Minister trickles seed from his fingertips into their cage. He addresses Magnus over his shoulder.

'You need to find a new role here, Magnus. Earn your keep a little.'

A job? Magnus could farm, perhaps, maybe teach maths or physics. Do some forestry. But he's leaving in four months. Whatever he contributed would hardly be worth it.

The Prime Minister glances out of the window at the rain, as if his next statement holds no interest. 'We can't send you home, Magnus.'

Magnus at first doesn't hear, doesn't understand; or rather he hears and it doesn't make sense. But the PM says nothing more, waits, blandly adjusts his cuffs, gazes neutrally out of the window as if they have an eternity before them, which in a sense they have.

When, after several seconds, Magnus grasps that a decision has been made without consulting him or, presumably, his home planet, his mind somersaults in horror: he has no money, is utterly dependent on the kindness of others, is a guest, a visitor, an immigrant. Aerth sent five astronauts. Four of them died. Going home was a promise, an undertaking. Promises can't be broken. It's unthinkable, unimaginable.

The Prime Minister walks to his desk, sits behind it, moves the phone, straightens a pen, doesn't look up. 'Matters of state take precedence, you understand. We're obliged to provide peacekeeping troops to areas of conflict around the planet, there are wars on our borders, and you'll no doubt be aware, closer to home, of the difficulties within our health system and the appalling state of education.' He smiles briefly, leans back in his chair, looks up at the ceiling. 'The country would ask why a foreigner – for that's what you are, Magnus, foreign – why a foreigner should have billions spent on him when the poorest have nothing.'

The room wheels in a dizzy, sickening vertigo; the colours, rich reds and blues and golds, blur and whirl together, faster and faster.

'I have to say, too, that I am personally, shall we say, healthily sceptical about your background. Your profound lack of modern scientific knowledge has been a red flag to many across the world. In any case, wherever you come from, whoever sent you – and we'll find out, sooner or later – Greater Britain will no longer be supporting you financially.'

Magnus clings to his coffee with icy fingers, fighting the urge to let it fall, stifling the impulse to drop to his knees on the deep pile carpet and keen with grief. The betrayal is like a wild animal consuming him from the inside, devouring his heart, his mind, his sanity.

The Prime Minister appears not to notice his distress. 'I have a proposal, Magnus. I expect to continue in office for many years to come, and I expect your full support, utilising your extraordinary, and to my mind incomprehensible, popularity.'

Magnus looks up. He hears contempt and distrust, recognises that a deal is being offered, understands that he has no bargaining power.

The Prime Minister continues. 'In return, you will receive a modest stipend to cover living expenses, a bit of travel, nothing extravagant. This is my personal offer to you, you understand. You'd be foolish to refuse.' The Prime Minister smiles again. 'So that's agreed. Splendid.' He stands, takes a black cloth and flings it over the birdcage. The canaries fall silent.

Maybe it's terminal

Magnus develops a longing to see home that pierces him like a knife in his heart. Most days he wakes sobbing. Most days his breakfast sticks in his throat. Most days he vomits.

He also knows that when you pull a knife from deep within the flesh, sometimes the wound heals. Sometimes you die.

Stranger in a strange land

Edward leans back in his chair, his fingers steepled. He has the same corner office as before. Magnus now recognises that offices like these, with windows and views, are given to senior people.

‘Refugees—’ Edward begins.

‘I’m not a refugee,’ says Magnus. He gives an exaggerated shrug, raises his eyebrows and smiles. His face feels as if it might crack with the exertion of smiling. He imagines a fissure extending up under his hair, breaking open his skull, revealing not his brain but his tender soul.

A nameplate sits on the desk. EDWARD THOMAS, PSYCHIATRIST. Perhaps patients sometimes forget who they’re talking to. Perhaps Edward Thomas sometimes turns the nameplate around to remind himself of his own name. Magnus understands that feeling and for a moment feels sympathy for the state of mind that would give rise to that kind of amnesia.

‘I came here of my own free will. I was…’ He pauses, the better to emphasise his next statement. ‘I was excited to come. I was. I was excited.’

Edward nods.

Magnus continues to smile with his aching face. He takes a breath, leans forward to ask about pills, but Edward speaks.

‘Displaced persons have a deep trauma connected with exile from their homeland. Particularly after bereavement.’

In the minutes when Magnus says absolutely nothing and stares out of the window at the silver birch which is beginning to shed its December-yellow leaves, the psychiatrist watches him. Magnus doesn’t want to be watched. He doesn’t want to talk about his past, his future, or his present. He wants Edward to prescribe him sleeping pills, anti-anxiety medication. Helpful things.

'I'm not bereaved.' Magnus turns his attention to the other window, through which he sees tall dirty-grey concrete buildings with long, blank windows like arrow slits, and high cirrus cloud against a grubby blue sky. He imagines streams of ice particles flowing inside the cloud. He imagines himself surrounded by frozen cloud at the top of a hill. A freezing fog. He realises viscerally, desperately, that he may never feel cold again.

'Loss, then.'

Magnus shakes his head. 'I've gained more than I've lost.' He stands, his eyes on the wispy clouds. 'A whole new world! Buildings, concerts, travel. Food! Music!'

'People?'

Magnus doesn't answer.

Edward Thomas rises too, comes to the front of the desk and stands right by Magnus, close enough for Magnus to feel the warmth of his body. Magnus beats down the longing to throw himself, weeping, on the man's shoulders. Instead, he fixes his gaze on the beige nylon carpet, on his shoes, which need a polish, on the laces, thin strips of rough-edged brown leather. When Edward speaks his tone is soft, gentle, sympathetic. 'You've lost your team, Magnus. Your family. Your whole world.'

Magnus walks to the door, leans his forehead briefly against it. 'All I want is to sleep.' He opens the door and steps into the unlighted corridor, his soul pouring out through the widening crack in his head.

Recognition

Magnus books a driver to take him up the motorway one muggy Saturday when rain is forecast. Rock music vibrates from the stereo, the beat thudding through Magnus's bones. Thrilled to have extra hours and a free lunch, the young driver bangs his hand on the steering wheel, yells along with the band, nods in time with the bass, while Magnus slumps morosely in the back, watching a landscape newly familiar yet somehow very wrong.

No massive oak forests. No deer, rabbits or squirrels. No grey wolf slipping between trees. No brown bears ambling along invisible paths. No elk, no shaggy red cattle, no wild ponies. No wheeling flocks of birds.

As for the Urthian wildlife documentaries, the kind thing to say about those is they're wishful thinking; nostalgia, perhaps; old footage, definitely. Not lies, no.

They speed past parched motorway embankments, where straggly bushes perch precariously on dead soil and withered grass. Beyond lie expanses of potatoes or maize enclosed by thin steel fences, ringed by thousands upon thousands of identical boxy houses. Occasionally a medieval tower rises above the roofs and Magnus's heart skips a beat.

Magnus has lost his appetite and is now dreading lunch, the pretence that he's hungry, the obligatory walk afterwards in this hideous place. It's not easy to find the historic pub in the village centre; they weave around chicanes along the traffic-calmed roads, park the car in a narrow, bendy road lined with dormer bungalows, almost blocking someone's drive, use the driver's phone to navigate the five-minute walk.

This isn't home. It's like any other suburb on Urth: cul-de-sacs, double yellow lines, convenience stores, a supermarket on the approach. Twenty times the size of Meriden back home. Noisier, smellier, dirtier, the streets lined with vibrant plastic litter and shards of glass.

The pub is hidden behind a parade of plate glass-fronted shops, its mismatched architectural features cobbled together like pantomime scenery: beige brick walls flanked by black timbers and white plaster, a steel flue, a stone chimney, diamond-paned windows, a wide wooden porch…

…and the doors, such familiar doors, doors he could draw blindfolded in his sleep: the double doors, carved in heavy black oak, of the ancient Moot Hall of Magnus's childhood.

Magnus stares at the doors, which seem to shimmer and ripple, somehow iridescent on this cloudy day. There's a sound too, which he's not sure if he's hearing or imagining: a faint musical hum, a long, swelling chord. The driver has gone in, is already at the bar holding a menu. Magnus hesitates. He places his hands on the doors, feels their solidity, knows they are real, fears for his sanity.

The driver turns, waves, grins. If Magnus leaves, the driver will have to pay for his own lunch. It's unlikely he can afford it.

Certain that nothing good can come of passing those shimmering doors, Magnus decides to ask for a meal to be brought out to him, will eat it at a picnic table. He steps away from the porch, beckons the driver.

A violent crack of thunder vibrates through him and the rain starts without warning, its weight and volume terrifying, like a waterfall. Without thinking, Magnus dashes inside, is assailed immediately by a nauseous faintness and a trembling which starts at his feet and rises through his body like a wave. He stumbles, grabs the back of the nearest chair and glances around to orientate himself. The dark wood panelling and maroon carpet are hazy, as if viewed through a smeary window. The atmosphere is close and stale, laden queasily with decades of fried potatoes and meat pies. Magnus feels he could cry.

But there's a woman sitting alone at a table by a window, and she's familiar, more-than-familiar, although he knows they have never met. Her face is framed by wild curls, freckles are scattered across her nose and cheeks, her eyes are blue and sparkling. She looks up at him with an expression of enquiry, followed so swiftly by recognition and joy that he knows that she knows who he is.

If you don't look too close (this is perfect)

Lying half-asleep on a recliner in the hot shade of a copse of slender trees, savouring the tart sweetness of local beer on your tongue, gazing drowsily at a smoky moon rising in a hazy sky as dry leaves drift around you, you can almost believe you're lying in your parents' garden.

You hear the car before you smell the exhaust; you hear the engine thrumming at the wide five-bar gate. You raise yourself on one elbow, ready to rise and open the gate, but Ruth leaps out of the SUV and the gate is swinging back against the small apple tree you have planted perhaps a little too close and you wonder, sleepily, if it may be possible to move the tree without damaging the roots; yet Ruth has already climbed back into the vehicle and is driving through with a burst of gravel, and now you smell it, you really do, the acrid and bitter fumes from the burned diesel.

Ruth slams the car door and trots across her plastic lawn with shopping bags full of shoes and tops and swimsuits for this sultry weather, to make the most of it before the thunderstorms arrive in the middle of August; she brings gossip from her friends and family and the village – not a village really, not the way you class villages; this one is far too big, ten thousand people, and it's sprawling, collapsing across the farmland, smothering the soil like it's fainted under the weight of itself – and she brings also an invitation to dinner in Birmingham next weekend, which you can tell she's excited about. Ruth loves to socialise, and that's not a problem.

And she leans down and gives you a kiss, upside down, says she must go and change and what shall we do for dinner, and you smile, and she smiles back, and you feel warm and happy, complete, at last content in this strange life in which you find yourself, however that happened, and that's a long story; and you know that by some miracle you and your beloved have found each other, and you dismiss the glimpse of something foreign, something alien, peeking out from the depths of Ruth's eyes, something that does not understand you, does not comprehend who you are, the worlds that separate you from each other, the space between you.

You two should meet

Everyone wants Magnus to have a drink with James the veterinary surgeon, the man who looks like Magnus. People want photos.

Magnus can't explain his reluctance without sounding weird, or scary. So he says nothing, but for months he avoids anywhere where James might be, for the sake of not being party to the destruction of the planet. Or universe.

Yet he's curious, too, wonders how much they share, whether their DNA is identical or whether they merely resemble each other, like this planet and his home. He ponders the likelihood of similar interests, attitudes and tastes; acknowledges in the deepest, most hidden part of himself that he would love a friend. At night he walks the quiet fields to the vet surgery, peers in the windows, imagines another life that might have been his; imagines the two of them together, brothers. He avoids testing the resilience of the universe even if its ending, hypothetically, might be a fizzle rather than an explosion. *Pfft.*

He's happy now, anyway, with Ruth. It would be such a waste of happiness.

Ruth and Magnus enjoy long suppers, long mornings in bed, movies and parties, and visits to her friends and family, where she shows him off like a prize, all fitted between his global trips. They get a kitten. Magnus maintains the small, neglected garden, plants blackcurrant bushes, hides the insecticides. Ruth shows him her favourite country walk: along the lane, skirting a laurel hedge, through a rhododendron thicket and a half-acre of conifer plantation, before they hold hands and leap a muddy ditch behind the shops.

Magnus can cope with the inadequacies of Ruth's understanding of nature on this nature-challenged planet, but he fears, irrationally, that the shimmering pub doors may act as a portal to his own world. The one time he asks Ruth if she sees what he sees, she points to a red admiral butterfly, so rare that it's worthy of note.

Over several weeks Magnus experiments with the doors. He wears sunglasses but still the doors shimmer. He approaches the pub from the side, his face averted, hears the hum, walks away. When actually entering the pub is unavoidable – Ruth has many friends she wants him to meet – he walks in behind her, his eyes closed, and feels again that queasy light-headedness, that unsteadiness in his legs.

Magnus comes to an accommodation with the shimmering doors. The shimmering is imagination, the disconnect between here and home causing a parallel disconnect in his mind. The alternative is a brain tumour, and he's not going to think about that.

Losing Aerth has been worthwhile, in the end. Magnus and Ruth have found each other, after he and Tilly lost each other. In his night-time dreams his lover is always Tilly. He can't admit this. Nobody wants to be second best, after all.

We can't afford you for to cook too often

It's cheaper to buy ready-made meals. Magnus disputes this, strides off to the Meriden butcher, where he stares at overpriced oxtail, tripe and chicken wings in the window. On the greengrocer's shelves are wilted cabbages, soft onions and a lot of tinned stuff. Even the dried beans are costly. Magnus thinks back to better meals, can't imagine where all that excellent food came from.

In one of the supermarkets he buys cakes and bakes, meals and deals, strolls home under a blazing sun, thunderclouds gathering in the west.

Wildwood

Magnus and Ruth have been snapped by paparazzi in London, but not yet in Meriden. The house is private enough, most of the time, surrounded by cracked fields, transparent hedges, and scattered shrubs not large enough to be called trees: tired field maples, a blackthorn, a bullace which should have yielded small round yellow plums last autumn but had none when they went with a basket to pick them. Not enough insects, Magnus had said, and they'd stared sombrely into the dusty scrub, seeking invertebrates.

He can't remember when he last saw a bird, despite the seed and the water he puts out each morning; but today – dark, cloudy, hot, threatening rain, already thundering some miles away – a wood pigeon alights on the tiny apple tree he planted last December. Magnus's heart leaps. He opens the door silently, creeps out from his cool kitchen into the heavy, humid air, crosses the plastic turf, desperate to see this wonder. As he approaches, the bird plummets to the dust.

A vehicle draws up. A car door slams. Magnus doesn't look up. He stoops and lifts the bird. It is warm and floppy in his hands. Its neck droops over his laced fingers. Its eyes are half-closed and dull. There's no heartbeat.

As if the pigeon's departing soul has sent a final message to the nearest living creature, Magnus experiences an immediate gut-churning desire for the wildwood, long gone, unobtainable, the living forest which once extended for miles in all directions from where he stands right here, right now; and perhaps it still does, in another world, another universe: the cool earth breathing beneath the outstretched arms of oak trees, that temperate rainforest canopy which holds animals, birds, insects, fungi and lichens, so much life; and he has an even more desperate longing for his childhood, when it was nothing – *nothing!* – to see flocks of thousands wheeling across the sky, to be woken by deafening summer birdsong at 3 a.m.; when it was normal to plant far more than the village could possibly consume because of what the birds would pick off.

Tears well. He sobs once, twice, sobs that contort his body and wrench his throat, sobs that twist his face and squeeze his heart. He drops to his knees, clasps the pigeon to his chest.

'Dead as a dodo,' says a man. 'Shame.'

Magnus looks up into the face of a stranger peering at him over the gate.

'My wife's a big fan of yours,' says the man. 'Astronaut. Environment, campaigning, all that.' He pauses. 'We saw you on TV last week.'

Magnus nods, lets out his breath very slowly, breathes in equally slowly, blinks back tears.

'Don't often see birds around here,' adds the man. He looks vaguely towards the spindly trees. 'I was going to ask for a selfie, mate. But you're busy right now, I can see that.' He glances at the bird crushed against Magnus's shirt. 'I'll come back.' He raises a camera, stares at the screen, touches a button. There are several quick flashes. 'Thanks,' he says.

Magnus looks down at the pigeon splayed against his chest, one wing dangling, stiffening, the other folded beneath its body, its feathers somehow glowing in the gloom: dove grey, pewter, charcoal, white, the palest pink, iridescent green and vibrant purple. He lowers it gently to the ground.

By the time he has brushed the soft down and the sharp grit from his hands, the lane is empty, the man has gone. The air rings with silence.

Devastation

The night of his birthday he's at the pub when a magnitude six earthquake strikes, and the world bucks and quivers like the wild thing it truly is.

Magnus lies bruised and stunned on the floorboards, covered in chunks of plaster, trying not to inhale the choking dust as he considers his position, both literally and morally, his gross lack of responsibility, his deliberate ignoring of possible – no, likely – no, definite – consequences.

If Magnus had not had one drink too many; if, finding himself behind James at the bar, he had refrained from experimentally reaching out through the shimmering air towards the man's shoulder; if – feeling, as he did, the earth waking beneath his feet, trembling, twitching, and shuddering – if he had instead turned and leapt across the rippling floor and out of the pub; if he had staggered along the undulating road until it calmed and settled, nothing would have happened. No earthquake, no destruction of village houses, no loss of life.

Who can he tell? They'll tease him, they'll mention the fracking a mile away and suggest a holiday or a visit to the doctor, despite everyone knowing there's some mirrorverse thing going on, that he actually (if they choose to remember) has travelled from this planet's twin; but on reminding them of his origins he's always been greeted with affectionate joshing and has felt somehow diminished.

He crawls dust-coated through the wreckage, plaster and grit in eyes and hair, bleeding from palms and knees and chin, fearful of helping with the rescue in case he inadvertently touches the wrong man, knowing how he'll be viewed.

Now this

Magnus spends a morning walking towards and away from the veterinary practice.

Closer: more trembling in the ground, more shock waves. Closer: more tingling in his body, like an electric current. Further away, in the housing estate on the other side of the road… nothing. A mile seems a safe distance.

Aside from the beard, which James wears and Magnus doesn't, he and the vet are mirror images. Magnus has no doubt that if they were to stand naked side by side, they would find the same moles, the same scars, in perfect symmetry.

Locals believe the shuddering waves which daily rumble and groan through the earth like the rolling of the sea are caused by fracking. Magnus knows better. Today he rides the rollers like a surfer, swaying loose-limbed and upright on the surge, grass and mud rippling beneath him. The swell subsides as he reaches the gate at the top of the field, and all is quiet, save for his juddering heart.

At home he tells Ruth that he believes it's too dangerous for him and James to ever meet; he feels they might be drawn inexorably to one another, like magnets, and that, once drawn, they would merge into one. Or the opposite: they might merge and cease to exist. Or worse: together they might cause the universe – both universes – to explode or implode or otherwise be terminated.

She puts her hands on her hips, regards him for a long moment, says: 'You really think you're something, don't you?' Then she laughs, cups her hands either side of his face, and kisses him.

How to contain a tragedy in eight easy steps

1. One emergency caesarean.
2. One little baby girl, who stopped moving, possibly yesterday.
3. One memory of a day, long ago, when Tilly's father broke similar news to you, gently, compassionately, physically. You wept, locked together in grief, under the oak trees. You remember the birds stopped singing and the woods fell silent, but that's probably your imagination.
4. One girlfriend, who frowns, licks her lips, opens her

eyes a crack and squints at you. Her face is blurry and unfocussed. Probably the anaesthetic. Or perhaps it's your broken heart.

5. One revelation. Ruth has never wanted children, she says, lying in her hospital bed, while you hold her hand, stroke her wild frizz back from her forehead and kiss her gently. She weeps: soft little sobs escape through her compressed lips; single tears squeeze through her scrunched-up eyelids. You beat down the thought that it seems for all the world as if she knows that this is how a bereaved mother should look.

6. One request. The doctors would like to perform an autopsy on the child. They are more interested than compassion should allow in the father being an off-world astronaut; they're interested in solar radiation and earthly diseases.

7. One refusal of permission. From you. And from Ruth. That makes two.

8. One secret. No confession needed, no revelation about your family history. You can start over, the two of you, self-sufficient and self-absorbed and self-centred and selfish. It's all fine, never been finer.

Alien

Magnus has become used to the sceptics, who smile and nod, or shake their heads, still smiling, and say, 'I believe you, thousands wouldn't!' Or, their smiles turning almost to sneers: 'Jammy'; or 'Nice work if you can get it'.

These people turn up everywhere: the pub, Ruth's family gatherings, schools, supermarkets, radio studios. Usually they're men.

Then there are those who tell him outright, to his face, that he's a liar. What's in it for him, they want to know. He used to respond earnestly, explain how Aerth and Urth can't see each other or communicate directly due to their positions either side of the Sun; that he's not part of a massive scam, despite his fame and global significance; that, far from being a millionaire, he subsists on a small allowance from the government; and yes, he'll be going back to Aerth at some point, he's not sure when (a tiny lie which sometimes gets people off his back). He learns to smile blandly, to brush past people with microphones or placards or sheaves of paper.

And there are the (probably) insane. Those who believe he's some sort of supernatural being – a god, or angel, or alien. Well, this last is true, but he's definitely not a shapeshifter. He had to look that up.

Women want to cosy up to him, hear the details of his life on Aerth, are obsessed with his love life. Some grasp his face, plant kisses on his lips, grab him around the neck and attempt to drag him into the crowd to dance or smooch. He can't deny that he's flattered, but he has Ruth, sometimes on his arm, most often alone at home.

He rarely visits the flat in London these days, rarely stays overnight. His driver takes him straight to Meriden, to the slightly fresher air and to Ruth's arms.

So it hurts when, one night, Ruth asks him where he really comes from. It's three in the morning and she has waited up for him, watched him online, seen some of this evening's pop-star madness.

'You know where I'm from,' he says, bewildered.

'Yeah, right.' Her voice is tired, flat. 'Forget it.'

The heart of it

One sultry afternoon, while making love, Magnus whispers Tilly's name. Ruth pulls away from him mid-kiss and demands an explanation, and he can offer her only the truth.

'I don't believe this, not for one second,' she says, and clambers out of bed. She marches into the bathroom and turns on the shower.

Magnus leans his forehead against the locked bathroom door and pleads with her to come out. He can explain, he says. She walks and talks like Tilly, has the same laugh, the same crooked little finger which she broke as a child when she fell off a horse, and the same mole under her left eyebrow.

He doesn't add that she also has Tilly's wild red-blonde curls, Tilly's ringlets at the nape of her neck, and she smells like Tilly, that mix of rose and musk. This seems, well, too personal. But what are the chances? In an infinite universe, what are the chances?

Ruth comes out of the bathroom, pushes past him and

rummages in her chest of drawers. 'So why have you never mentioned her?' She turns, still naked, and looks him up and down as if she hardly knows him.

Magnus doesn't know why not.

She dresses quickly, gathers a random selection of clothes and jewellery: knickers, socks, her favourite silk shirt, jeans, lacy nightwear, bracelets, bangles, necklaces, earrings, and drops them onto the rumpled bed sheets.

'You're hard work,' she says. 'With your moods, your depression.' She spits the next words: 'Your *morality*. Your *walking gently*, your *truth*, your *listening to the bloody heart*.'

She stands on tiptoe to reach her blue rucksack down from the top of the wardrobe and crushes the clothing into it.

'Don't,' she says. 'Don't try to stop me.'

He wasn't going to, but he's had a few glasses of Beaujolais and doesn't quite grasp what's going on.

'Tell me,' she says, 'where you met this girl. That's all I want to know.'

'We were teenagers. We had a baby. The baby died, like our baby died.'

Ruth snorts and marches into the bathroom.

Magnus pulls on a pair of shorts, picks up his shirt from the floor and wipes his eyes, which sting with the effort of not weeping for the babies, for the wildwood of his youth, for his first love.

Ruth stamps back into the room, stuffs shampoo and toothpaste and conditioner into the rucksack and slings it over her shoulder. The bathroom door crashes against the side of the bath and swings shut with a solid, final clunk. She retrieves her shoes from under the bed.

'They even looked alike, the babies.'

Ruth turns abruptly, her face, her voice, her finger accusing him. 'It's always about you,' she says, her voice tight and high, then she's out of the door and running – *running* – down the stairs as if she's been waiting for this occasion, this opportunity, as if there is an arrangement in place, something she is running to.

The better man

'Bears!' yells Magnus.

James stands at the other end of the field, which quivers beneath their feet. He bellows back: 'Sorry?'

'What do you know about bears?'

James lifts his hands, palms upwards, shoulders raised, the universal sign for *Nothing*; or *I don't know*; or *What are you talking about?*; or *The man's a lunatic.*

The field rumbles. Trees sway, a hedge trembles, the ploughed furrows in the mud ripple like waves on a swelling sea.

Magnus retreats, satisfied. He opens the gate and reels down the lane, lurching over the billowing concrete. They could have been friends, he's sure, if the physics hadn't been against them, if the matter and antimatter particles weren't so appallingly incompatible; and he imagines that if the tables had been turned, if James were to enter his, Magnus's, world, a world of bears and wolves and wild boar and mammoths, a world of snow and ice and forest, a world of low-tech needs-must decisions, with a loaded rifle by the back door, the vet wouldn't get on very well at all.

Urth sucks

Urth is a quicksand that threatens to swallow him without trace. Nothing is as it seems. People never say what they mean. They obfuscate, hint, negotiate obscurely. No wonder there are so many wars.

And Ruth – Ruth! Ruth and James. They knew each other as teenagers. That first day in the pub, she thought he was James.

Magnus belongs nowhere, can't go home, doesn't want to stay here.

He reins in the loneliness, the disappointment, the grief, the fear, pushes it deep inside, tamps it down, layers it under the concrete of the cynical realism he's beginning to acquire.

With the benefit of hindsight

Magnus's regrets – too many to count – come to him in night visions when he lies alone and wakeful in his London flat.

Don't look back, never look back, urge online advice pages: *Regret nothing.* Yet Magnus feels he has been constructed out of memory, regret, love, fear, hopes and dreams; he fears that if he follows this advice, his mind and his heart will empty and he will cease to exist.

His inadequacies hold him in a kind of stasis, a paralysis in which opposing forces (hope and fear; love and fear; joy and fear) trap him like liquid mud that sweeps down in landslides and solidifies around whole villages: men, women and children, dogs, cats and mice, caterpillars, ants and woodlice, locked forever in the place where they were taken by surprise.

At night he rolls from one side of his bed to the other, seeking deliverance from the heat of regret, seeking a cooler space for his body. His bedroom windows are open to the searing breeze, which is desiccating and deceivingly soft, and are screened against the mosquitoes which nightly gather on the thin metal mesh; they sit lightly, patiently, waiting for him to absent-mindedly open up and lean out for fresher air.

Desperate to communicate with Tilly, he records videos which may or may not reach her, looping as they do back and forth across the solar system via strategically placed satellites around Urth and Mars, waylaid by solar storms, locusts and other hazards. It's become a kind of addiction, a need which some days relieves his despair. He sends her news, the blandest of news: how his tomatoes are doing in the London smog, the long-standing injury to his big toe, his ongoing tennis lessons. Occasionally he hears back; she mentions once that her husband died years ago, and sends kind little messages asking about his life and his friends, and his heart breaks anew.

He'll never meet her again, never take her hand or kiss her cheek, because there's no money for space travel, what with wars and natural disasters and trade agreements that have to be serviced somehow; and on a cost–benefit analysis there is no benefit at all to any nation on either planet in sending a lone middle-aged astronaut millions of miles across the solar system.

In the deepest loneliness he confides his lack of friendships to a door attendant, Jack, in his building, and finds himself invited to spend Christmas Day with Jack's family. They're Hindu, but they love Christmas, and whatever the rumours about Magnus they are magnanimous enough to invite one more guest who really won't make any difference to the catering. Magnus needs to find gifts for twenty-eight individuals. The old terraced house is stuffed with tinsel and presents, and people of all ages eating and drinking and playing games, and Magnus loves every minute: the chaos, the noise, the music, the corny movies; the Indian sweets, the mince pies, samosas and turkey; the arguments, tears and laughter, and the trading of gifts between cousins; and he eats way too much so – in self-imposed yet corporate penance, because everybody does it – he takes part in Veganuary, jumps on alcohol-free Thursday and sugar-free Monday and meat-free Wednesday and seafood-free Friday and caffeine-free afternoons and evenings. Later in the year come Maycation, Blue-Moon-June, Movember and many other events. He embraces them all.

He writes his memoirs, a lyrical retelling of his childhood on Aerth and his adulthood on Urth, including for tact's sake his astonishing good fortune at being able to travel from one world to the other, mindful of the PM's support. Parts of the book are almost truthful, and it sells moderately well. He gives twenty-eight copies to Jack's family.

Over the years, he records videos for Tilly which he doesn't even attempt to send, in which he tells her urgently and passionately that he loves her and he's always loved her and forever he will love her. Sometimes he cries.

He imagines how she might react if he turned up at her door; he imagines her surprise and joy, her uplifted face, her warm embrace. But sometimes, in his imagination, she sends him away. He is not welcome, she tells him, and never was, and his youth rises up to suffocate him.

Multiple choice yields more accurate* results

The children sit cross-legged on the floor and gaze up at Magnus, interplanetary traveller *(astronaut, spaceman, extraterrestrial*)* and special guest at their end-of-term assembly *(speech day, prize-giving, sports day*)*. They don't fidget, are on their best behaviour, their eyes intent as they study him, their faces luminous with hope *(excitement, joy, anticipation*)*.

Magnus is quite a coup: one of the governors *(parents, teachers, local dignitaries*)* knows someone who knows someone who knows his assistant(s) *(colleague, boss, minder, fixer, chauffeur, bodyguard, friend*)*, and the fact that the assistants get to see people they know two hours' drive away is a bonus. Magnus doesn't speak Hindi *(French, Japanese, Luganda*)*, but an interpreter is always on hand.

His heart feels like it's splitting in half, from the permanent ache *(tenderness, bruising, agony*)* in his chest, which doctors tell him is nothing to worry about, and perhaps he should try yoga *(herbal sleep pills, relaxation tapes, a hobby*)*. He imagines cracks radiating from a central fissure, along his ribs, down his arms, cracks that, given time, which he has too much of in any case, will fracture his whole body *(mind, soul, courage*)*.

But he'll give these young optimists a memory to treasure. It's the least he can do. He'll smile as he walks through school. He'll let them grab his hands *(touch his clothes, pat his arms, tell him jokes*)*, he'll give them autographs and selfies.

Magnus has his little upbeat speech by heart *(it's the heart of the matter, the crux of things*)*: three minutes on his unique upbringing, three more on the marvellousness of theirs, and in the last four he tells them that everyone is special *(you all have gifts, your appearance doesn't matter, you don't have to do what other people tell you*)*. He responds to carefully curated questions from the more biddable students with answers he chooses at whim, almost. Coffee with senior staff *(teachers, educators, facilitators*)* and half an hour to admire the classrooms *(gymnasium, children's artwork, bicycle racks*)*. He could do this in his sleep, and in many ways he does.

The assistant stands nearby, waiting to whisk him off to the next engagement *(meeting, drinks party, press conference*)*; they ooze confidence, radiate fun, would be ideal for this job, yet they've never travelled off-world, and it's Magnus who, anxious in crowds, fiercely self-critical, and the sole point of contact between two planets, was born millions of miles the other side of the Sun.

In the car *(taxi, helicopter, tour bus*)*, Magnus contemplates the likelihood of a nap *(coffee, swim, movie*)*, followed by a simple supper enjoyed alone in his hotel room rather than dining with local officials *(actors, politicians, captains of industry*)*.

Later he'll find a perfect heart-shaped leaf *(pebble, shell, sweet*)*, slipped into his pocket by a young admirer, which he'll place gently on his bedside table alongside his one photograph of home.

*(*Delete as appropriate)*

First, do no harm (3)

His TV interviewer is smiley, charming, flirtatious. Magnus meets her in an office with long squashy sofas in lime green and orange, where they sit knee to knee and go over her questions. She pours white wine into generous long-stemmed glasses, and offers plates of cheese and olives, a bowl of strawberries and a platter of chocolate cupcakes with cream. She and Magnus laugh a lot, despite his feeble jokes.

He tells her about his new work in schools, where he teaches children how to grow vegetables, and how to reduce pollution and look after the planet. He plans to write a children's book about how he travelled to Urth in a spaceship.

They walk into the studio, relaxed, like old friends, and wave at the audience, which is clapping with enthusiasm. Magnus claps back, six slow claps, his hands raised before him. Then he clasps his hands and shakes them high in a little victory salute.

An assistant places wine and a selection of snacks on the low table between the lean black leather armchairs where Magnus and his interviewer sit. Magnus is so at ease that he takes a strawberry as the live prime-time interview begins.

'Magnus Ovarden, let's leave aside, for now, the continued speculation about your origins.' She glances, archly, at the audience, who titter. 'Tell me about your recent work with schoolchildren.'

Pausing only for a second *(as he registers the neat dagger between his ribs, as he flushes with quiet fury, as he forgives her)*, Magnus pulls in his growing paunch and covers his stomach with his jacket while he speaks at length about his food education programme, which will tackle both obesity and malnutrition. They've covered this in the office. It's like working from a script.

His interviewer becomes inattentive, gazing at him without focus as she touches her earpiece and nods once, a movement so slight it's almost imperceptible. Magnus's comments peter out and he forgets to mention his fundraising appeal or the next stop on his national tour. She doesn't notice: she's consulting her tablet, her neatly manicured forefinger swiping left, right, down.

'You've heard of the recently published and highly controversial work on hereditary viral infections?'

Magnus nods, although he's not heard a thing; this is off-script, not approved, not even hinted at in the pre-interview. But he doesn't want to look ignorant. He wants to look like he belongs, like he was born here.

The interviewer leans forward and smiles, gazing into his eyes. Magnus leans forward too, distracted by the faint shimmer of eyeshadow on her upper eyelids which seems to match her eyes, a beautiful grey-green, and he smiles back, ever so slightly tipsy.

'You've told us many times, Magnus, that there are no secrets on Aerth.'

He nods. Yes, this is true. There are no secrets on Aerth. There never have been secrets on Aerth. 'Yes, that's right,' he says, and his smile becomes broader. Dinner, maybe more.

She consults her tablet again oh-so-briefly, and he admires the way she hardly has to check her facts, the elegance of her posture, the sense that she's a woman who knows what she wants, and gets it too.

'What do you say to the accusation that viruses have been used as a weapon of war on your planet?'

His mouth opens in surprise. While he absorbs this reversal, this species of betrayal, the fact that this was not – most definitely not – discussed in their meeting, his brain whispers old, old words at him, words he first heard without understanding as a young child: *First, do no harm…*

'That viruses were first deployed in the seventeenth century?'

Another whisper: *Listen with all your heart…*

'That the deadliest virus, the one still in circulation, was used against Aboriginal peoples in the eighteenth and nineteenth centuries?'

Walk gently…

'That whole populations have been eliminated by this virus?'

Live truth…

'That your two great pandemics were in fact caused by this weapon of mass destruction?'

Love…

Magnus becomes dimly aware of his shallow, rasping breaths, and the way he must look: foolish, unprepared. He closes his mouth, tries to swallow, but his throat's dry. His heart's thudding, and he has a sudden and desperate urge to leap over the coffee table, to run out of the studio and crash through the double swing doors and push people to the floor and flee the building and run, just run, just run.

'That your planet's philosophy of life, the five rules, the pacifist lifestyle, the matriarchy, Magnus, these are a response to the terror of wholesale planetary human destruction?'

Phrases from his childhood hammer in his mind, powerful phrases that run through him sinew-like, ingrained, automatic, providing tensile strength for each day, every day, every moment, every bloody day on this bloody planet.

FIRST, DO NO HARM!

'That your race is heading for extinction?'

LISTEN WITH ALL YOUR HEART!

'That your Mars programme is an attempt to start a virus-free colony?'

WALK GENTLY!

'That your planet has agreed to allow colonies from our planet, with a view to repopulation?'

LIVE TRUTH!

'That this offer will have benefits for our own planet, which, as everyone admits, is overpopulated? So the record will show that, after its appalling history, your planet is at last being generous?'

LOVE!

The interviewer pauses, opening her palm to indicate that now, now that he's been punched in the stomach several times, she would like him to reply.

Magnus clears his throat, places his trembling hands between his knees, only half-conscious of the hot sweat running down his back and his face, his pounding heart, his nausea. He hears, as if a long way off, laughter, and booing, and his interviewer asking calmly for a doctor. A roaring begins in his ears, and a darkness encroaches on his sight, his vision reduced to a tunnel in which he can see his inquisitor leaning forward, holding his hand, her face a study in compassion.

With an effort Magnus pulls back. Questions vie for attention – *Is any of this true? Hasn't Urth had its own genocides? Aren't there gaps in history Urth never refers to?* – but in the end he asks only one. His voice is hoarse, almost a whisper. 'When was this announced?'

He was never a Boy Scout but believes in being prepared

Magnus likes to keep certain items in his pockets, even though he's forty-five and lives in exile on a foreign planet. You never know when something might be useful.

- ✦ Binoculars, for birdwatching, and for keeping an eye on the concreting-over of fields, sewage outflows, trees being grubbed up, tornadoes, fracking activities, and the smog that lies over everything like an infection;
- ✦ A notebook and pencil (ditto);
- ✦ Nut-and-chocolate-filled energy bars, with extra protein, in case he's trapped up a tree by security guards and fierce dogs;
- ✦ Reading glasses, so he can see the notes he writes;
- ✦ Three almost-spherical pebbles, perfectly smooth, which he tumbles in his fingers like worry beads for no reason, or if there is, he doesn't admit it;
- ✦ A letter from Tilly, creased and fragile.

Think global, act local

Well, it's a lark, in a way. Scurrying under cover of darkness over fields, through wire fences, a rucksack filled with tools clanging on his back. If he could blow up the fracking fields he would, but that kind of immense explosion could destroy whole towns of people sleeping in their beds. However far he has drifted from Aerthian ways, he cannot bring himself to kill, even by accident. Instead, he breaks into offices, smashes computers, pours sugar and sand into fuel tanks: small hindrances that make him feel better and cost many thousands to fix.

People invent stories, as they always have

Always, always, it's Magnus whose picture makes the news, surrounded by followers he never wanted, invited or expected. They share food, take turns sitting up at night as sentinels. The army gets called out. Police circle in copters. Drones gather footage. The crowd traipses along highways, traffic diverted.

He attempts to disperse them with various statements, true and untrue, anxious not to lead yet another Urth movement. There are already enough. The one thing he ever led was the Aerthian expedition, and look how that turned out.

I'm no leader. I'm an ordinary bloke with an extraordinary story…

I come from another planet. Please leave me alone…

I'm a fraud, I grew up in Tynemouth, my family's waiting for me…

People talk with him and at him, planning a better world: peace, equality, reversing global warming. Better housing. A one-tier health system. More trees! Cleaner rivers! No smog! Abolish war, abolish politicians, give everyone a pig and some chickens, an acre for all.

They invade supermarkets, storm warehouses for clothing and footwear and tents, remaining tidy and polite at all times, putting unwanted items neatly back on shelves. Some give interviews, explaining their philosophy which is, apparently, based on Aerthian values. None of these are familiar to Magnus. They include lying naked on wet grass at dawn to obtain planetary energy, mystical rituals learned from ancient mentors, and hibernating in caves. When Magnus explains that there are no rituals and that Aerthians prize kindness and live peacefully alongside nature, he is greeted with cheerful agreement, and ignored.

Meanwhile there's Aerth's history. He wishes it were a vicious rumour, but nothing else makes sense. It must be the truth. He wants to run, hide, heal his deep wounds, but there is nowhere to go.

He attempts to escape his admirers, but they follow, eager to draw him into discussions of angels, telekinesis and reincarnation. Trapped one evening on a motorway bridge, invited to levitate above the streaming traffic, he finally loses his temper and punches someone, and is arrested and locked up in a cell for the night.

Magus reflects on his behaviour. His mother would not have approved. Hilden would have encouraged him to behave differently next time. He is torn between his desire to keep the peace and his growing anger at Aerthian concealment of its murky past. Yet there is nowhere he would rather be than back on Aerth.

Released the next day, he is greeted ecstatically by chanting crowds.

The trees break his heart

Urth thinks cutting down trees is progress. Urth thinks a heating planet is irrelevant. Urth believes Magnus is merely a sideshow, that his Aerthly perspective adds nothing. Magnus's anger surges like a volcano.

Accompanied by diehard activists he climbs trees *scheduled for demolition*, where he lives day and night, food winched to him on pulleys, until he himself is felled by tranquilliser darts.

Magnus chains himself to vulnerable trees, is dragged away, stands over their corpses later and weeps. Sometimes there are green shoots on the felled timber, signs of life in even the oldest and sickest trees. He picks them, throws them to passers-by as he's dragged into security vehicles.

He digs damp holes like a fox's earth in tiny woods, refuses to leave when the bulldozers roll in.

Eventually the diehards drift away. It's hard work with no reward, not even a few minutes' fame, or money.

In the news, again

Walking past a newspaper stand at lunchtime, papers heaped on the ground in piles, rained on, discarded – and oh, the waste of paper, the murder of trees – Magnus once more sees his photo on a front page. This time it's *The Spotlight: Daily Gossip, Daily News.*

Astronaut imprisoned for criminal damage

Astronaut Magnus Ovarden, who crash-landed in the North Sea nineteen years ago, once again spent a night in police cells after taking a pickaxe to a mining machine.

The 49-year-old, who remains unmarried despite several high-profile relationships, was subdued by seven police officers who were forced to administer ketamine.

Sergeant John Smithers, 38, said that Commander Ovarden is unusually strong for his age and build, and speculated it was because of military training on Aerth and Mars. When pressed, Sergeant

Smithers admitted that he was sceptical about Commander Ovarden's background. 'The Mars photos look like Utah or somewhere like that. The forest pictures could be from a hundred years ago,' he added. 'It's easy to manipulate images. All I can say is that the commander is highly trained.'

Commander Ovarden's solicitor, Erin Tackard, 23, who qualified earlier this year and is being paid by the taxpayer, said that speculation was unhelpful. 'Commander Ovarden is a citizen of Urth,' she said. 'We should concentrate on the wider picture, environmental damage by big corporations. For the record, Commander Ovarden's home planet Aerth is pacifist and has no armies.'

Commander Ovarden is believed to have taken Urth citizenship eleven years ago. He has always denied spying for the purported planet of Aerth, despite its apparent lack of modern technology and its rumoured societal and medical problems.

A minority of astrophysicists and security specialists have formed a coalition to investigate Commander Ovarden's credentials. Experts believe Ovarden may be in constant contact with his handlers. An expert in cyberwarfare, who wished to remain anonymous, said on Friday that the commander's mission may be 'the thin end of the wedge', but declined to be drawn further.

Speaking on an encrypted line from Brasil, Jan Musgrin from Urth First, the banned ecological pressure group, described Commander Ovarden as a pioneer and a 'contemporary hero'. 'The tragedy,' Musgrin said, 'is that we have only 70 hectares of Brasilian rainforest left. Commander Ovarden is a great supporter of our work, and clearly believes the time has come to make a stand.' Musgrin denied having any further knowledge about Ovarden's background.

Magnus Ovarden faces charges of trespass, aggravated assault, criminal damage and resisting arrest, along with other members of Siblings of the Urth. These charges carry severe financial penalties as well as jail sentences, although the latter may be waived because of previous good character, particularly given the current crowded prison conditions.

The Home Secretary was not available for comment.

Playing by the rules

After his twenty-fifth arrest Magnus is conveyed long-distance overnight in a police van together with his wire cutters, balaclava, night vision glasses, petrol can, matches and cereal bars. He sits in the front and chats with the driver, who otherwise might fall asleep, he's that tired.

They stop for coffee at an all-night service station, peruse the newspapers together, and buy milk chocolate and low-fat potato crisps, hot chilli flavour, which they share on the way.

In the grey light before sunrise they arrive at a country estate behind high stone walls. It nestles in a valley of bleached treeless fields and is a haven of ancient oaks, cedars, rose gardens and wide green irrigated lawns.

He knows this place. On so many occasions he was a guest of honour, a unique guest, the only off-world astronaut alive. He often showed visiting presidents around the estate, finishing with the Prime Minister's menagerie of local wildlife, a byword for conservation, much discussed in the press but not seen by journalists: a mangy fox; nondescript birds including a robin, three blackbirds and a bedraggled barn owl; a weary badger; a family of mice; two rats; and a small pond for frogs and newts, although Magnus has never observed any. He spoke eloquently, passionately, of the need to conserve species, while fearing inwardly that it was already too late, and was warmly applauded and congratulated on his deep knowledge of wildlife.

Today he feels truly alien, a specimen to be examined, kept at arm's length, safely under lock and key, controlled, not wholly accepted, never truly understood, and he simmers with resentment in the warm crimson and scarlet dawn. It's like a blindfold has slipped off, revealing that the world's leaders, of all people, are willing to damage, disregard, trample, deceive, hate. His protests, criminal damage and arrests are the sole things giving him respite from the words clamouring inside his head: *DO NO HARM... LISTEN... WALK GENTLY... BE TRUE... LOVE...* The contradiction works, somehow, in some mysterious way cancelling out his agony. He sleeps better in a police cell than in his own bed; his persistent hope each night, as he drifts off, is that the Prime Minister will decide at last to send him home.

The driver saunters off to the house. The caged fox stares at Magnus, unblinking, insolent, as he leans into the unlocked van for the wire cutters.

Terse and humourless, the Prime Minister gives Magnus precisely one minute and fifteen seconds, excavated from his schedule.

'You seem determined to undermine me at every turn, Magnus. I have run out of patience. You can return to wherever you came from.' He raises a hand to forestall Magnus's inevitable response. 'From now on, you're on your own.'

He is, himself, immune from homesickness

Over dinner at a café he notices a video playing on the TV. It's Ruth, and it's gone viral. He feels his life give way beneath him.

I watched him for years... He's definitely not an alien. Not that I'd know what an alien looks like. He's exactly the same as you or me.

Not a spy, no. He's not that clever. And he's hopeless with tech.

Yeah, his English is perfect. Just the weird accent.

I don't know really. Iceland? He really likes cold weather. Could be Iceland.

Mentally ill, I think. Needs to be at the centre of things.

Oh yes, he believes it. He thinks he can destroy the world. Yeah, bonkers.

He turns up at a hostel for working men but without work is ineligible. He tries a homeless hostel and is laughed at. He tries a migrant hostel but is not foreign enough.

It's getting dark; curfew begins in two hours. Magnus walks back to his old apartment building and looks up at his top-floor windows. It looks like a fortress, and that clearly was what it had to be, back when he was famous. Now he is merely infamous. There's a soft whine above his head, and he looks up to see a security camera swivelling in his direction. A voice speaks. 'Better move on, sir.'

Sir.

Magnus walks to the park. It's locked. He circles it. Spiked railings, too high to climb. The park-keeper stands at the gates, staring. A car passes, long and sleek, its windows blacked out. Probably someone he knows. This is how he used to travel, curfew irrelevant.

There's a fluttering in his stomach as he contemplates a night outside. He walks another hour, reaches a residential area, stares into people's lighted front rooms. Someone bangs on a window, shouts. Startled, he scurries off down the street.

He puts up his jacket hood, then lowers it. No need to overdo the suspicious bit.

A patrol van slows, stops. Without a word two officers take him by both arms and shove him into the vehicle, already half-filled with homeless. The stench makes his stomach heave. A man leans forward, taps him on the knee. 'Don't hide behind bins,' he advises.

Magnus opens his mouth to protest, realises it's pointless.

A smelly, crowded, subterranean room; thirty-seven filthy men, plus Magnus; two open toilets in the corner, one tap, no towel; bread and black tea at 6 a.m.; the streets. Somehow his money disappears overnight. And his phone, and all his socks.

Do you know who I am?

An officer looms over Magnus, who's sitting on cardboard outside The Emporium, the place where *simply everyone* goes to buy clothes, books, shoes, holidays, dinner. No one stops. He's grimy and dishevelled, smells a bit, and the beard doesn't help, but their sideways glances tell him that most passers-by know exactly who he is. Many once called him their friend.

Knowingly, with a wink, he tries the immortal line: 'Do you know who I am?'

'You could be the King of Sheba, mate. You can't sit there.'

'Queen,' murmurs Magnus.

'Makes no difference to me.' The officer taps a small, colourful badge on his body armour. 'Diversity training.' He hauls Magnus to his feet, says, 'You can come quietly, or move on. Your choice.'

Magnus sways. He's not eaten for a couple of days. His ankles hurt. He keeps his head down, unwilling to reveal his vulnerability, the possibility of tears. 'I'm the astronaut,' he says quietly.

'Yeah. Let's look at you.'

Magnus raises his head.

'Difficult to tell, mate. Anyhow, we all know it's been a giant scam. Very clever. Brilliant, in fact. But the game's over, mate. C'mon.'

Magnus resists, flattens himself against the plate glass window. A crowd is gathering, devices out for photographs and videos to post online, and Magnus thinks *Not again* as the officer pulls him, drags him to the waiting vehicle, twisting those ankles, and he cries out in pain.

A chant arises: *Spaceman! Spaceman!* Someone shoves him from behind and he topples against the security vehicle, grazing his forehead. Being driven away is a relief. He counts blessings... well, he's out of the weather. He might get breakfast.

At midnight he is summoned upstairs. He braces himself at the thought of being released during curfew, but a woman stands there, someone with whom he once had a brief affair. She smiles at him and he recoils a little, certain that he must look disgusting. 'I know him,' she says, and bestows her luminous smile on the officer. 'It's Commander Ovarden, fallen on hard times. Could happen to any of us.'

At home she feeds him real cheese and ripe fruit and expensive oatcakes, offers him fluffy towels and a shower, insists he can stay as long as he needs, and, more grateful than he can express, he falls with her into bed.

Days pass blissfully, restfully. He begins to hope this could be permanent, that life could smooth itself out in comfortable anonymity, that he could work at something humble, like street cleaning. He can't pay his friend for her hospitality but he cooks and cleans, runs errands.

Now and again people come to interview him, film him. Despite his broken heart, his emotional bruising, he revels in being taken seriously again, giving his honest opinion on everything from music to politics to interplanetary travel, his old Aerthian instincts hampering any sense of self-preservation. Without restraint he criticises the Prime Minister's decision to render him homeless, a deliberate policy of neglect, perhaps in the hope that Magnus would disappear or perhaps die. The PM, he states forcefully, is a conspiracy theorist, and doesn't believe that Aerth exists. The PM, he adds, is deluded, and power-crazy, and corrupt.

One evening he's chopping and mixing dinner ingredients along with a TV chef and several million others, only half-listening, preferring on the whole to do his own thing. He turns to the fridge for the faux chicken. The adverts begin. He hears his own voice above an ominous soundtrack of discordant violins. Magnus spins around, shocked, sees his own magnified face, hears his own echoing words. The title comes up. It's a prize-winning documentary, *The Fallen*.

It could be, he understands, a pun on his falling to Urth. But he needs only seconds to know that it's a hatchet job, a cruel lampooning, lumping him with loons and con artists. Another spotlight has been turned onto Magnus's life on Urth, illuminating the murky spaces, the cracks, the dirt. He doesn't own himself, and perhaps he never has.

Ad break over, the chef continues, but Magnus opens the kitchen cupboards, surveying their contents like a naturalist on new terrain – *chickpeas tinned tomatoes apple puree cinnamon mustard sardines garlic seaweed powder quinoa chocolate cupcake mix honey anchovies rye crackers marmalade baked beans oregano passionfruit juice* – then tips it all into one glorious casserole in a magnificent never-once-used cast-iron dish, which he slides into the oven at two hundred degrees, before washing the wooden spoon and wiping down the surfaces. He piles the recycling neatly in a corner.

Then Magnus quietly gathers his stuff, places his door key on the kitchen worktop and takes the lift to the street below, where he plunges into the throbbing, crashing, hooting, thieving, wailing, weeping night.

A door stands open

More days, and some nights, on the street. Hunger, thirst, profound discomfort. The distaste of passers-by. The occasional kindness of strangers.

A door stands open. A church, tall and imposing, decorated with carvings and statues. Magnus has attended events in churches but has never entirely understood them. From inside comes the sound of a piano, followed by singing. Not many voices, maybe a dozen, but oh, what beauty. Pure, long notes, a melody that crosses between parts, that takes unexpected leaps – minor sevenths, fourths, moving between keys. He's never heard anything like it.

Magnus steps closer, peers inside. The pews are empty. The small choir stands close to a grand piano at the far end. He counts the lines of music again; he can hear seven lines, then five, then four again, but now it's six. There is no vibrato; the voices are cool and clear, youthful, and alongside them the piano flows like a shallow, pebbly river, notes rippling.

Magnus walks inside, drops his bag at the end of a pew and sits. He closes his eyes, the better to hear this unfamiliar music. Bass voices take the melody; then tenors take it higher, without strain. The voices remind him of bees humming in woodland, bears waking from winter sleep. His mind drifts; in his imagination he gazes up, watches treetops swaying in the singing wind. Curlews soar above, their long cries and bubbling song harmonising with blackbirds and thrushes and wrens and nuthatches and skylarks, piercing his heart with their joy. The curlews sing louder, more urgently, more beautifully, imparting some important message he is not clever enough to decipher. He sits at the base of a majestic oak tree, close to the tumbling river, and sleeps.

He is startled awake by a gentle hand on his shoulder. The music has stopped. Unable to bear the end of the dream, Magnus sobs once, his sob echoing in the silence. A kindly-faced old woman is sitting beside him. She hands him a tissue.

Magnus gathers himself, asks when the concert is.

'They're recording.'

'Oh. Did I ruin it?'

She shakes her head, smiling, and he is reminded of Hilden. 'Do you need food? Somewhere to stay?'

It's obvious that he does. Obvious that she has no idea who he is. Her kindness is impersonal and generous. He can't answer; his throat is constricted by gratitude.

She takes his grubby arm and walks him to a cafe, where she buys him a baked potato with plant cheese and salad. They drink coffee. She asks him about his background. He can't tell her. People might hear, and life is difficult enough right now.

He mentions his identical twin James, who lives in the Midlands and is good with animals. They like to go down the pub together on a Friday night, wear each other's clothes, mix it up for an always appreciative audience. They're musical, James more than him; they sing duets and people drop money into a beer glass for the pleasure of seeing them perform. Which they donate to charity. 'It's fun,' he adds bleakly. The lies come easier these days.

'My advice to you, Ryan, is to make it up with James. Whatever has driven you apart isn't worth it, you know. And here's some money for a hostel.'

She takes him to the door of a place that Magnus knows is full. He's nervous for her since curfew is approaching, but she turns at the end of the narrow alleyway and waves, smiling.

Magnus fingers the cash in his pocket. He stares up to where stars should be, then at the ground, notices a dandelion flowering in a crack in the concrete. Useful, dandelions. Nutritious, medicinal, deep-rooted, tenacious.

He shoulders his bag, turns north-west.

Inevitable

The trees sway slightly as if in a breeze. There's a kind of rumbling, like distant thunder. Magnus has not eaten for two days and feels distinctly shaky.

He buys a cheap bread roll, stuffed with mush that smells like tinned dog food. He eats it sitting on a low wall outside the shop, watches people's faces as they pass, wonders if anyone recognises him. He's almost out of cash.

After eating, he walks on. He chooses a narrow lane leading away from Meriden towards fields. After a few minutes he stops by a five-bar gate. The surgery is tucked behind a wispy hedge at the bottom of the field. Magnus climbs the gate and stands between rows of potato plants. The day is damp and warm, muggy. Sweat soaks his hair and his shirt. Perhaps he's ill. Perhaps this is where it all ends for him, a heart attack in the middle of a field on a planet very far from home.

Magnus takes a breath of diesel-tainted air, removes his jacket, immediately feels better. He drops it with his bag among the potato plants, has a sudden urge to feel the soil beneath his feet, discards his shoes and socks too.

Urth quivers under his bare soles. The thunder seems closer. The hedges are swaying in the hot, humid breeze – back and forth, back and forth, wider and wider. His tender feet stumble over jagged stones. He stubs his right big toe, looks down at the blood oozing onto the pale, parched soil. He doesn't ask himself what he's doing here, how he may be received, what he expects to happen.

More rumbles. Not thunder. Urth grumbling a little.

He eases himself through the gap in the hedge, jogs over the burning-hot tarmac, reaches the front of the building and opens the door.

Ruth is behind the reception desk, filing, her back turned.

The floor trembles. The calendar on the wall sways very slightly.

'Woah,' she says. 'Big one today.'

She turns, smiling, then sees it's Magnus at the door. Her eyes widen, her smile disappears. Magnus closes the door behind him, walks across the reception area and into the consulting room.

'Wait! Stop!'

The rumbles continue, closer, louder.

James looks up from the examination table. Beside him is a small woman, a toddler in a pushchair and a bright green budgerigar in a cage.

‘Hi,’ says Magnus.

James doesn’t seem surprised. It’s almost as if he’s been expecting this visit.

The room shudders. A pane of glass in the window shatters. The woman screams, grabs the pushchair and rushes out of the room as Ruth runs in. She darts between Magnus and James. ‘No! Whatever you want, no!’

Cracks appear in the walls. Medicines fall from shelves.

‘We need to leave,’ says James. He opens his arms to herd Ruth and Magnus out. Magnus doesn’t move. He wants to stay here, for ever, just him and James.

There is a rumble far beneath them. A ripple appears under the blue linoleum. Magnus and James watch it flow across the room. It meets the wall and disappears under the skirting board. The wall quivers, then settles. There is the sound of another window shattering.

‘We need to leave, Magnus.’

The pain in Magnus’s chest feels like his heart is being ripped apart. He can barely breathe.

The floor ripples again, in deeper waves, like the sea. The waves keep coming, building.

They brace themselves, roll with the motion. The bookcase by the door topples.

James says, ‘What do you want, Magnus?’

Magnus can’t speak for longing, for love and pain, for regret, for admiration, for joy and sorrow. Tears run down his cheeks. He waves a hand vaguely, shakes his head, tries to smile but his mouth won’t.

‘I know,’ says James. ‘I know.’ His eyes are kind, as if he’s talking to a client whose pet is terminally ill. He steps towards Magnus, his arms still open – in surrender, or embrace, or shepherding.

‘NO!’ shrieks Ruth.

Outside the door there’s a crash, then another. It sounds like the ceiling’s falling in. Magnus looks up, remembering another ceiling, years ago, when the pub collapsed. A crack appears above their heads. Fragments of plaster land in their hair.

Ruth shoves Magnus in the chest, shoves him back against the wall. The wall shudders, sways. The ceiling sags above them.

I deserve this, thinks Magnus. Probably. He pushes forward from the wall, back into the centre of the room. A second later the wall collapses behind him, breeze blocks and chunks of plasterboard hitting him on the shoulders as he ducks towards James and Ruth.

Ruth screams into his face, a long, vibrating screech. She’s no longer furious. She is beside herself with terror. She screams again: ‘Keep away!’

James takes Ruth by the shoulders, moves her away from Magnus. They stumble together over the debris like some four-legged alien creature, hunched and deathly white with plaster dust, only their eyes and mouths alive.

James turns to Magnus. They can barely see each other through the dust in the air. It’s dry, catches in the throat, makes them cough.

James steps through the dust and rubble towards Magnus,

his hand extended, like a friend. Behind him Ruth snatches up the metal desk lamp and brandishes it like a pickaxe.

Helpless, weeping, Magnus feels himself pulled into James's arms. The relief is immense, a feeling of coming home, that he is finally where he belongs.

They hold each other tight, chest to chest, cheek to cheek, their breathing slowing, their pulses synchronising, and James shuffles Magnus towards the door, while around them the world is ending, and Ruth bashes Magnus over the head.

On the one hand. On the other.

Convicted as a terrorist, without the right to defend himself in court, Magnus is confined to an offenders' hostel in East London. A low-cost, fully automated and secure solution is the only acceptable answer after the millions that have been spent on him. It has been decided that he is a threat to the integrity of the planet.

Magnus no longer cares where he is. He's had enough. Nothing holds his attention for long, unless it's a plant, or an insect, or a bird. He can stare at these for hours; he looks almost brain-damaged, he overhears someone say one day while he gazes at the markings on a dead wasp.

He is not to go more than half a mile in any direction from his small single room. He is microchipped and must check in at the hostel four times a day. He has a small allowance for food and sundries. For clothing or shoes he must apply in writing. He must walk everywhere. He's permitted occasional calls and visitors.

Nobody calls or visits.

There's a paved yard, surrounded by high walls. He obtains permission to create a couple of raised beds at his own expense. He begs half-rotten timber from local builders, steals some from a skip, buys seeds and compost instead of shampoo and phone credits.

Magnus becomes expert at raising tomatoes, peppers and aubergines, which still feel exotic to him after a childhood in which these were too frost-sensitive to be grown. He plants a tiny apple tree, which blossoms beautifully but produces no fruit until he pollinates the flowers himself with a child's paintbrush he finds on the street. If he'd wished, he could have sold each apple for a large sum, judging from the prices in the shops, but he keeps his small harvest in his cell-like room and remembers Aerth when he eats them.

After the first year he thinks about expanding his small domain, maybe sharing his produce with other inmates. He could try lettuce, spinach, rocket, herbs, all fast-growing. But they want to hang out in the yard, kick a ball, smoke, waiting out their short sentences. Magnus himself has no chance of being released.

He occasionally muses about this twilight life, that it's deemed better than complete annihilation.

It depends on your perspective.

Home is where the heart is

Several armed officers come to the hostel, accompanied by turbaned men with guns. After security checks, they take him to the garden of the Indian Embassy, where now he gazes at the spindly birches struggling in the cracked clay soil, attenuated wispy things with few leaves. Whip-thin branches litter the ground, dry and brittle, crunching underfoot.

The Ambassador speaks, but Magnus barely pays attention. His mind is on his aching feet and legs, the insomnia that wakes him at three in the morning, his inability to get back to sleep. Close at hand a bird sings, a few notes, half a song, a phrase cut off before its ending. It might be a blackbird, from the liquid beauty of its music.

'As you know, India's far ahead of everyone else, Commander Ovarden.'

'Mm-hmm.'

'Our progress has been incredible, I have to say.' The Ambassador pauses, seems to weigh his words. 'I have been informed we'll be ready in a couple of months. I am instructed to ask if you wish to join our mission?'

Magnus stops. 'I'm sorry, Ambassador. I don't follow.'

'To your planet, to Aerth.'

Magnus stares up into the treetops. Beyond the fragile tracery of branches and leaves hangs the sun, pale red in the thick, yellowy air. 'I can't see that bird,' he says. 'They're always more difficult to spot than you think.'

'Commander. No other country is anywhere near this close to interplanetary travel. Some are still trying to launch satellites.'

'And what's in it for you? For India?'

'There are many reasons. For instance, India wishes to be the first Urth nation to send a crewed craft the other side of the Sun.'

'I'm fifty-three,' says Magnus. 'Out of condition. Space flight could kill me. That wouldn't be great publicity.'

The Ambassador makes an impatient noise, a sort of tut. 'Then get into shape.'

Magnus ignores him. 'I've been here too long. And I just don't want to. Do anything. Any more.'

'Well, Commander, it's up to you, of course.'

'I'm thinking of writing a children's book.' He peers into the branches. 'There it is,' he says. 'It's a mistle thrush.'

The Ambassador doesn't look for the bird. He watches Magnus. 'Magnus,' he says. 'You would be doing Urth a kindness if you were to leave.'

Magnus continues to watch the bird, the thrush, its shape and its music so similar to those of a blackbird, but not a blackbird. You could never mistake one for the other, not if you place them side by side, not if you really look at them, really hear their song.

Mapping the ages

Had Magnus never desired a life of excitement and adventure, an escape from ice-age Aerth, he would not now be sitting under sacred trees at the very edge of a mountainside retreat in northern India, Urth, contemplating the ravaged landscape below. At six thousand feet, the temperature is pleasantly warm, but the heat haze on the horizon produces a shimmering of colours and shapes. It reminds him of something, but he lets the thought drift away.

The terrain below is laid out like an ancient map, distances and geographical features notional. Towns and villages lie flattened in this smoothed land, its yellow, black and red soils swirled into each other as if still liquid, its roads and rails delineated as if by pencil. There are no trees, vehicles, people or livestock. Rivers remain vigorous, solid, their courses altered and widened. The floodwater ran down this vegetation-denuded mountainside, miraculously bypassing the retreat, and gathered itself into an unstoppable force. Today, and for months past, there is drought and deadly heat. It would be sensible if nobody ever lived here again, but the Empire holds nearly three billion people, and land is too precious to waste.

Within a month he'll be travelling to Aerth, his longing for home stronger than ever. Never mind the philosophy that says you can never go back, that nostalgia is not a good reason to return, that people move on, that you yourself change too much. Despite his fears of what awaits him, and his quiet expectation of death, he is determined to try.

Magnus sits quietly on the mountain as day gives way to dusk. Night falls slowly, bringing a chill, and he shivers. He looks up. Above the Urthian smog, here where the air is clear, stars are visible. He hasn't seen stars for years.

Love

Aerth Orbit

Landscapes roll beneath you in vast expanses of coloration, like butterfly wings, chameleon skin. Green and blue – no, emerald, sapphire, like jewels forged deep in rock.

Or… hues of olive, lime, forest, moss, spinach, kale, pine, spring leaves, new grass, kelp, carrageen, fresh climbing bean.

And… teal, peacock, flash of jay's wing, kingfisher, cornflower, borage, grey-blue-green, slate, iron, sand, granite, desert, terracotta, black.

Even… white, so brilliant it's dazzling, painful on the eyes.

Gaze on continents, islands, lakes and seas. Swoop like a hawk, glide like an eagle, skim never-ending forest, dive through windows of rock towers. Float over billows and breakers, swirls and surges. Ride air currents along golden beaches, stretches of shingle, precipitous cliffs.

Contain, just, your excitement as you rise on thermals above the steepest, most inhospitable mountains. Plunge to hidden valleys, lush with water and ferns, insects and joy.

Bear witness to shoals of fish, packs of sharks, dolphin herds, whale pods. Comprehend the gigantic animals of the Amerikas – giant bears and elefants, armadillos and ostrich. Thrill to the sight of millions of khulan racing as one across the central plains of Asia. Adore the parakeets, the puffins, the penguins. Worship the albatross.

Weep. Laugh.

Love.

Intermission

The spaceship crew look exhausted, shocked, cold, the way you feel. But there's no crash-landing this time. A gentle glide across Thetford Forest, a controlled deceleration along the new runway.

There's nobody you remember at the Space Agency, nobody familiar among the welcoming faces. They speak to you as if they know you, introduce you to young astronauts in training. There are no crowds, no dignitaries, no journalists, no battalions of cameras and microphones. Your face is not beamed across the world. Those who receive you are quiet, polite, gentle, as if you have merely returned from a few days away.

After a hearty meal in a warm dining room and a speech of welcome, which you acknowledge with a smile and a few words of thanks, you pass the night in a guest cabin, grateful for your layers of new woollen clothing, for the comfortable bed, and for your window onto trees and stars and sparkling frost.

The people at the Agency hope you'll stay a week or two, to share your knowledge and unique experiences. But you can't, not this time. Something tugs you homeward.

You leave at dawn, take the Hostel path through the forest. No one stops you. They are confident in your promise to return.

At each Hostel you eat one meal, don't speak, don't stay. Rules and guidelines don't apply to you, and perhaps they never did. You are outside all worlds.

Wrapped in a blanket, you sleep on the hard, cold ground under the black night. You listen to the small, scurrying sounds of hedgehogs, mice and voles; the slink of fox, the prowl of wolf; the unhurried pace of elk and moose and bear; the chitter and growl of badgers. You lie perfectly still, your eyes closed, and let them examine you, their whiskers and fur soft against your face and hands, their scent pungent, untamed. Owls and nightjars and nightingales make music above you, the dark air ringing. In the grey dawn rabbits bound away, scuts white against the dark trees. And the curlews sing wild and high and free.

Inheritance

The house is exactly as Magnus remembers, and has (literally) dreamed, over months of travel. It nestles almost invisibly into the landscape, surrounded by the dense and sunless wildwood. Its turf roof is cropped by a nanny goat and her kid, who step delicately around the solar panels gleaming in the sunlight. The triple-glazed oak windows, the sturdy doors front and back, and the walls of the vegetable garden, currently laid to grass, are all in great shape. The forest has encroached on the orchard and paddock and imposed itself on the water meadows and fields. Young oaks, the acorns planted by jays, tower over hollies, brambles and hazels, dog roses and honeysuckle. The weir roars a mile away, louder than Magnus remembers, its turbulence a signal to leaping salmon and trout.

Ryan is there, waiting for him. He has received the messages sent ahead about the lone traveller, returned. It is midday, and lunch is laid – new bread, rich butter, wild berries, white and yellow cheeses from goats and cattle and sheep – and mugs are ready for tea.

Before embracing, they gaze at each other for a long minute, discerning their younger selves beneath the wrinkles, the grey hair, the heaviness of their older bodies. Forty years fall away, just for a moment, and they are once again best friends, growing up together.

Ryan takes Magnus by the shoulders and turns him to face the trees. 'Remember?' he asks.

They glance at each other and smile.

'Which one was it?' asks Magnus.

'Not the highest, you couldn't manage that. See the one that's half-dead?'

'Lightning strike?'

'Yes. Three to the left of that.'

The oak has grown, changed, but yes, there's the nook, there are the branches Magnus hid behind.

'I'll walk over later, see if I can get up there.'

'Beware the bears.'

Magnus laughs, but Ryan is only half-joking.

They sit on the low stone wall separating the garden from the meadow. A few goats with their kids graze the grass and wildflowers: scabious, knapweed, ragged robin, clover, and others whose names Magnus doesn't yet remember, their faces like old friends.

'I wondered if you would ever make it back, Magnus.'

Magnus takes a deep breath. It's almost like a sigh, but not a sigh. He can't get enough of this sweet air. 'I wondered too.' He glances at Ryan. There's no need, right now, to say very much about his time away. 'It's a long way, you know.'

Ryan nods. 'We got messages from you, every now and then. And then there were long gaps, and I wondered. Well. It would have been understandable if you'd decided to stay, settle down, have a family.'

Magnus closes his eyes, shakes his head briefly. He can feel tension centred in his solar plexus, beginning to spread. It makes him hold himself very still. He opens his eyes. 'I had some girlfriends.' He grins.

Ryan chuckles. 'Girls. I should have guessed.'

'But I always wanted to come home. And interplanetary communication is tricky. There are solar storms, things go wrong with the relay. Locusts!'

'Seriously?' And now Ryan is laughing, and Magnus feels better, and he laughs too, and holds at bay a tiny bit longer the depression and meaninglessness that marked his final years on Urth, that seem now to be woven into the very fabric of him;

and he's not so far removed from Urth that these might not overwhelm him in lonely moments, in the dead of night. But he can hold them back, today, in this fine sunshine in his childhood garden, the temperature a balmy twelve degrees.

'Have you seen any Urth videos?' Magnus asks.

'Some. A long time ago.'

'The thing is, Urth's not like us.'

'I wouldn't expect it to be.'

Magnus hesitates, then: 'It's overcrowded. Polluted. They want to come here, live here, you know.'

'I know.'

'And?'

'Let them. There's plenty of room.'

Magnus is about to raise objections, but falls silent. Staring at the forest, he remembers the high-rise apartments, the highways, the vehicles, the filth, the glitz, the hustle, the greed. The heat and smell of an exhausted planet. He closes his eyes, breathes deep, follows advice given him long ago, on both planets – *Let it go, let it go* – while Ryan waits, patient, oak-grained, steady in the winds of change, supple like a leaf.

Magnus of Arden, the youngest of ten, and by some miracle the only one alive, has inherited his parents' farm

Magnus feels younger than he ever did during his decades away. There's energy in the woods: pheromones released by trees for their own health affect humans too, and he feels his heartsickness falling away, a sense of well-being streaming up from the ground through the soles of his feet, into his body and his mind and his soul. He breathes deep, tastes the sweetness of air and the scents of plants and animals and fungi, the almost-forgotten fragrance of home.

He'll sleep in the house tonight, alone, despite Ryan's invitation to stay with him. There's food in the kitchen, a stove already laid to ward off the night-time chill, his old bed warmed and aired. It strikes him for the first time how lonely his parents must have been, with only each other and their one surviving child for company. The loneliness must have become unbearable in their later years. It makes sense now, their living apart. No shortage of love, but solid practicality as they entered old age, and a veiling of the pain they would otherwise see daily in each other's eyes.

He can't stay here. He'll find a young couple to work the land, raise a family. His imagination shies away from the possibility of no healthy children, persuades him to dream of fertile soil, fertile people, warmth and joy.

He plans to travel – *As if you haven't travelled enough!* said Ryan, bemused – but this time he'll be learning Aerth. He'll explore what it means to do no harm, how to listen wholeheartedly, how to walk gently, how to love and live truth. How to live a glad and joyful life. He wants to understand his planet's history, to write and read and dream, and convince people that hiding the truth, rewriting the past, however well intentioned, is like trying to breathe without oxygen.

He lights the stove, warms the food, wanders through the house, plate in hand. Memories arise, unbidden. He stops by the bookcase in the hall. Here are the old atlases, worn and frayed. They'd be collector's items on Urth, worth a fortune within some arbitrary code of scarcity. He lets the thought drift. And here's the handwoven rug in the sitting room, and the multicoloured shawl, draped over the sofa. And he'd forgotten the tiny window on the stairs, frost speckling its glass, a view onto moonrise.

He's no longer sure he can bear to leave. He'll wait a few days. Tilly's on her way, bringing two of her sons with their wives and children. Tomorrow there'll be music, and singing, and stories, and laughter, and feasting, the time-honoured traditions of all peoples, all cultures. Rooms not slept in for generations will be made welcoming and warm, the young families filling the rambling house. And Magnus's heart leaps with trepidation and joy.

The years don't fall away

At ten in the morning Magnus sits with Ryan on a bench in the sun, gazing at the forest, the birds, the busy insects, the old garden walls clad with spleenwort, tiny bellflowers and toadflax. Spires of foxgloves perch between stones, bumblebees crawling onto the spotted floors of the open purple flowers. He can't remember all the plant names, has been away too long. But it doesn't matter. Here he can breathe. Here his muscles are relaxed, his diaphragm no longer taut and tense. His breathing is slow and deep and regular. He might even nod off.

On the edge of his vision he becomes aware of movement – and there is Tilly, leading a horse out of the forest towards the house. Magnus suddenly can't catch his breath. He's not ready; he thought he had hours, thought she was coming this afternoon.

He stands. She waves. He waves back, wonders what they will say to each other when they meet. The horse is lame. Behind them come two young men, another horse, a wagon covered in canvas. And then there's noise, not only talking and horses' hooves and the creak of the wagon, but children squealing and laughing and running and being spoken to firmly by women – and then they are all upon him, surrounding him, smiling.

The young women shock and delight him by kissing his cheek as if he's a much-loved uncle, and the children do what children do best, getting under everyone's feet. He mucks in, lifting what he can off the wagon, allowing Tilly's strapping sons to do most. Ryan taps him on the arm, says: *We'll take the kids to the orchard, give them food, play with them.*

Magnus looks back over his shoulder at Tilly. They have still not said a word to each other, and he feels his trepidation increase. It's too apparent what forty years have brought each of them: hardship, work, life experience which has undermined the idealism of youth. In Magnus's case, too much alcohol and stress and pollution. Tilly has become round, like a little ball on legs, when once she was slender and lithe, a dancer, a rider, a runner, but she's strong still, and heaves a large wooden crate off the back of the wagon with ease.

He couldn't have lifted that crate. He lost weight for the trip home, stopped drinking, got into shape, but after months in interplanetary space he has lost muscle. Yet he's beginning to regain at least a modest zest for life, the tiniest joy at simply being. He hopes he will soon shed the remnants of cynicism, the carapace of self-protection he acquired while away. He imagines it like a suit of armour he saw once in a museum: he's taken off the metal plates protecting his arms and legs, the sabatons for his feet, the gauntlets for his hands – he can tread lightly, give generously – but his helmet and breastplate remain.

When the house is arranged to Tilly's satisfaction she comes to the orchard, seemingly untired, still fresh and strong. Magnus looks around for camouflage, a group activity into which he can melt, is about to say *I'll finish this story*, but Ryan and the children are no longer in sight. It's just him and Tilly.

Magnus tumbles three almost-spherical pebbles from one hand to the other, carried with him for what feels like the whole of his life. He can't quite remember where he picked them up: one, azurite and malachite, probably his favourite; the second, dull red haematite; the third, sandy beige. This one got dropped a while back, and is chipped.

Tilly sits on the grass inches away, her eyes clear, guileless. He briefly drops his gaze, unable to bear the pain of being seen. Is this friendship, or love, or a combination of the two? What can he offer, except the emotional distortion that arises from being squashed out of shape? But he's suffered worse pain than this over the years and has never been a coward, whatever else he's got wrong, so he raises his eyes and they gaze at each other, and now the years seem insignificant.

Tilly's brows furrow, briefly, her eyes questioning, then she takes his hand in hers, and kisses it. *You'll stay*, she says, and it's not a question but something akin to a command.

Magnus opens his mouth to protest, to give all the reasons he should not stay, should not contaminate this ancient and yet new-wrought home, but the word that comes is – *Yes.*

Acknowledgements

A huge *Thank you!* to everyone who has accompanied me on my writing journey.

My family, to whom I dedicate this book, and my sisters Sarah, Rebecca and Jodie, and their families. Over many years you have patiently listened to me talking about writing, and have read early drafts of this and other work, with kindness, encouragement and love. It means a lot.

Writing friends in Bristol: the Harbourside Heroes – Amanda Huskisson, Euphoria Kew, Val Powney and Katie Turnbull – thanks so much for our regular meet-ups over the years, where we talk about writing and so much more; members of the Bristol Climate Writers, especially Morag Shuaib and Caroline New, who read and commented on early drafts, and Kevin MacCabe; writer Nicola Keller, an astute reader and commenter; writer and mentor Michael Loveday, who has a particular love for the novella-in-flash; and writer and editor Jude Higgins, who runs the Flash Fiction Festival, where I discovered the wonders of flash fiction and first had this book longlisted in a competition. Thank you all for your support and encouragement, which I hope I have also given you.

I owe a debt to the many storytellers I have encountered in books, plays and movies (from Shakespeare to Star Trek, Austen to Asimov, and so many more); and to my parents, no longer with us, who instilled in me a love of reading and books of all genres. We were never without at least one book to read in quiet moments, and I keep up that family tradition.

My special thanks to Neil Griffiths and Damian Lanigan at Weatherglass Books, who picked this book for the shortlist of their Inaugural Novella Award; and to Neil, again, and Lamorna Ash, both brilliant and sensitive editors who really understood the story, at times even better than I did. I have enjoyed reading your own books. Thank you, Sarah Terry, for helping with the last fine adjustments to the text and for pointing up my writing quirks.

And Ali Smith, thank you. What a privilege for my book to be chosen as a winner by a writer of your calibre. I am still amazed.

AERTH

DEBORAH TOMKINS

First published in 2025
by Weatherglass Books

A CIP record for this book is published by the British Library

'Wildwood' was first published in a slightly different form in *Earth Hymn: KYSO Flash Anthology 2019* (KYSO Flash Press).

ISBN: 978-1-7395707-8-1

Cover design: Tom Etherington
Typesetting: James Tookey

Printed in the U.K. by CMP Books, Poole

www.weatherglassbooks.com

Weatherglass
Books